SYNAPTERGY

THOMAS MUROSKY

Published by World Where Press
State College, PA
www.worldwherepress.com

Synaptergy

First Printing 2020
ISBN: 978-1-7348398-0-7 (sc)
ISBN: 978-1-7348398-1-4 (e)

The Internet addresses in this book are accurate at the time of publication. They are provided as a resource, but due to the nature of the Internet, those addresses may change.

Commitment to Open Source: Word Where Press uses FOSS software where available. This book was produced with LibreOffice, GNU Image Manipulator Program, Sigil, Calibre, and the following open fonts: Charis SIL, BioRhyme. Audiobook edition produced with Audacity and Kid3.

LCCN: 2020935859

SYNAPTERGY

PART 1:
COMING ALIVE

1

The mechanical arm holding the laser emitted a low buzz as the targeting marker was aligned.

"Charging to fire!"

"Fire when ready," John announced. The laser began its focused boring while Mark shifted his eyes across the ceiling. "Twelve" he thought to himself. He tried to speak it, "Twelve lights...twelve lights...twelve," but he had not been able to say anything since last November.

"Can you feel anything, Mark?"

After a delay, a computer connected to the ACAT speech synthesizer relayed a robotic "NO".

During brain surgery the patient is kept awake so the doctors can communicate with him during the operation. This laser was busy boring a nearly microscopic hole in the top of Mark's now bald head to place the implant into the primary motor cortex. The implant itself was a low-power electrical device manufactured with two separate metal alloys designed to pull power directly from his body eliminating the need for batteries or charging. As for the function, that was more complicated. By interconnecting with synapses in the motor cortex, the company promised Mark that he would be able to relay his thoughts into controlling robotic limbs through encrypted short range networks. Though the possibilities were endless, Mark was intrigued by a small shot at somewhat normal life. He wanted to say something without this infernal computer or to pick up a glass of water; maybe his chief concern was using the bathroom without assistance.

"It's in! How are you feeling now?" John asked.

Again, a pause before the robotic voice disinterestedly mustered, "FINE".

The operation was complete, and now it was a waiting game for the device to set itself into position and begin the process of interconnecting with his neurons. If the rodent studies were any indication, the process would be complete in about ten hours, and the connections were best made if the subject rested. The twelve lights holding Mark's attention went dark as he eased off to sleep with the help of the anesthesiologist.

Mark woke up in a haze six months ago to bright lights and the bustling of people. His hazy vision slowly focused allowing him to vaguely recognize people he briefly met at his father's company get-togethers. In a split-second of panic, he recognized an operating room. He jerked his arm, but no movement happened. He was unable to wiggle a finger, unable to remember what landed him in this state. He knew he screamed, but no noise emanated from his mouth. He was instantly overcome with the most intense panic he ever experienced. Mark wrestled with how to get their attention; how to ask what happened. He was desperate for answers to questions he could not ask. Talking was always taken for granted, but now he was reduced to silence.

The battery of tests concluded that his mind worked perfectly, but his brain lost the connections to his major limbs and his mouth. The former complications meant parental assistance with every task Mark had learned for himself over the last seventeen years. Fortunately, the latter, his communication issues, could be solved with the aid of a computer and some simple training, well, simple for a robotics student. It was crude, but it accomplished basic communication.

Mark grew to hate that ugly ACAT computer. The computerized monotony that replaced his own voice seemed to stress every syllable in precisely the wrong place. Single sentences required a painful amount of time to generate; it was like asking a professional typist to use one finger to type a lengthy dictation. The ACAT device allowed for the bare minimum of communication, yet he could not express his deepest thoughts or carry out a meaningful conversation. Maybe that was for the better; he was too depressed these days to engage in life's joviality anyway.

While he slept off the last remnants of the potent cocktail of pharmaceuticals delivered by the anesthesiologist, Mark recounted the last six months of his life in his dreams, or were they nightmares? Those were one and the same for Mark over the last six months since he went from a senior in high school taking college courses to being a prisoner inside his own mind. His once flourishing relationship with his parents was cut short into one word answers, not because of teenage angst, but due to the loss of his voice.

He loved his parents, but now found communication difficult, and the relationship soured, turning into a holding pattern of simple words surrounding the most basic of needs. His once rich late night conversations with his dad turned into simple "YES" and "NO" and "TIRED" and "HUNGRY". He missed the times in the evening at the kitchen table talking about wild theories and future goals while he pursued an education in robotics. He missed the talks about how new breakthroughs in science could help in medicine (of chief interest to his father's occupation), but also in industry and wage-labor. Mathematics, physics, computers: the things that seemed all too normal to Mark while his peers were busy trying their hand at teenage foolishness. Since the fated day he woke up in the hospital, however, he has felt a strain in their relationship. It seemed to come from both sides; Mark only communicated his most basic needs because of the labor now required to talk. But his father seemed to have acquired a chip on his shoulder as if somehow blaming himself for what had happened to his son. Of all the people he missed speaking with the most, his dad was the top of the list.

The impact on his mom was worse. She always wanted to improve the conversation, receive feedback at home on sweaters, dinner, or feelings, but Mark was more mundane in his daily conversation with her. Their transactions were generally centered around needs. Not that there was any strain before November, but this stay-at-home mother took her role of meeting everyone's needs seriously. She was an expert at meal times, a fountain of wisdom for personal conflicts, and she would never cease to spin out blankets and scarves in her down times, each one personally crafted with love by the skillful twisting of her aluminum crochet hook. She always instigated excellent conversation, but her habit led only to sour rejection as her attempts to reach the fallen world in her son's mind was shattered with the same simple words—"YES", "NO", "TIRED", "HUNGRY", "TV", "READ". Now her only connection to him was the pleasing one-liners that came out when she read him his books.

His communication with his sister also suffered. He generally got along with Kristy. She would watch him when he was a child when their parents were able to leave them home alone to steal a few hours by themselves. In recent years, she married a wonderful young man who befriended Mark. The couple lived just across town. Mark used to spend Saturday evening for dinner and a movie at their house. The best part about his times with Kristy and Sam were the conversations. In that environment, a teenage boy can talk to his young adult sister about the tales of life with the parents, but the ACAT stopped all communication. The other conflict was his wheelchair. The porch steps at Kristy's house was as easy to navigate as a moat seeking to protect their house from his burden. Mark spent his last six months' worth of Saturdays brooding over his losses instead of going to their house. Not that he wasn't invited, but now he saw himself as an encumbrance to their time.

Mark's life devolved into more routine than he ever wanted. Early in the morning, the clock radio gently announced morning by giving him his other pleasure in life: music. He was a prisoner in bed, only being entertained by the morning DJ. Eventually, someone came to get him out of bed and he was taken to the bathroom, served breakfast, and then parked in front of the television while his mom completed the morning chores. Only the most basic of words were uttered in the whole process, and only those that were necessary. His loss of speaking destroyed his family; all the important conversations were over, and Mark could not make up his mind about whether he was more depressed with the loss of the use of his body, or if he desperately missed the people he saw every day but could not address in a manner matching his intellect. He was trapped inside his mind with his dreams and nightmares.

In his present, oft-repeated nightmare, Mark was seated at his place around the dining room table trying to talk about his day. He relived his last day at school and tried to tell them all about it. He tried to talk about his plans for the weekend, and about his new projects. He opened his mouth to speak, but nothing came out. Flustered emotions overcame him as he shouted louder and louder in his head. His parents did not respond. He yelled and screamed, but no response. They were talking to each other, completely ignoring him.

"LISTEN TO ME!!!!" He shouted at the top of his lungs, but nothing. The words were trapped in his mind with no way of escaping; no way of getting the attention of the people he longed in his heart to talk to. He finally burst out crying, but again nothing. Suddenly he awoke in an instant, panted a few deep breaths, then dipped back to sleep one more time.

2

Mark slowly awoke from his drug-based sleep to a quick cough and clearing of a throat. His mom's usual way of cough-clear, cough-clear was distinctive, so he knew it was her before his eyes silently shifted to the corner to confirm with his sight what he already knew in his head. His mom sat in a lonely chair tucked between the electric wall mounted heater and the white institutional window. Her long hair reached down past her neck, some at her back while some covered her breast. As was her habit, she was crocheting something. The pink yarn was being rapidly woven into a shape that he was not able to make out from his position. He could see her brown eyes darting between the pattern and the object being created.

For those of us who can talk, we understand the difference between saying, "hello," and thinking it. We can feel the difference in how our mind processes the request. But Mark has needed to intentionally move his cheek to communicate with the ACAT computer, so he had to put more direct force into simply saying hello. He felt helpless to talk without the computer. His eyes jetted around the room finally fixating on his belovedly-hated ACAT laying alone in the opposite corner, lifeless without his input. But out of seventeen years of ingrained habit, he voiced, "Hello Mom," with the simplicity he had the very last morning he audibly spoke to her. Without delay, a smooth young male voice echoed the exact words from his head, "Hello Mom!" It was neither robotic nor belaboring. It did not stress syllables in hard to hear places, but was natural and smooth.

Susan flinched, completely unsuspecting to hear anything in the room. Her eyes darted up, fixing on a black speaker just above Mark's head on a shelf out of his reach. "Mark?" she exclaimed. For a split-second, Mark had not realized the sound was real, but it was. He moved his head, the only thing in his body that he still controlled, to look into her eyes and attempted to talk again, "Can you hear me?" The speaker echoed the words as quickly as they flowed from his consciousness. "Yes!" she exclaimed, darting out of the chair, still holding the pink project. The yarn unfolded, falling from the bag, momentarily catching their attention. His eyes fixed to the tiny pink frame in her hand.

"What are you working on?"

Baffled, Susan held up a quarter-finished sweater, clearly for a baby. It seemed so weird to her that he would ask such a mundane question in light of the circumstances, but easy, causal conversation was the thing he longed for the most. He did not want to talk about hurt feelings or if he was in pain or about the operation. He wanted to know the little details in life he used to love discussing but were now too belaboring to attempt to talk about. He longed for the effortless conversations he had not partaken in since last November. Yes, "What are you working on?" is exactly what he wanted to know.

Ӂ

The trip from the hospital to the cul-de-sac was short and familiar. It was full of formerly good memories of coming home from visiting his father at work, but the last several months were replaced by driving to the hospital for a barrage of tests, surgeries, poking, and probing. He was glad to be out of there even though the most recent trip held more hope than the prior visits.

Mark tested the new speaker while en-route home. One block from the hospital, he thought, then forced the speaker to whine,

"Are we theeeerrrreeee yet?"

Eric looked at him through the rear-view mirror and rolled his brown eyes before spawning a subtle grin. This was the very first time Mark had said anything he did not have to say in a long time. Susan let out a laugh quickly followed by Eric. Mark gave his speaker a command through his thoughts to project an evil laugh. "Heh heh heh he" emanated from the speaker positioned directly behind Eric as if a tiny, creepy passenger was waiting to strike. It was truly amazing that the device could not only speak for him, but also reflect the tone and attitude he projected in his words.

Mark called out street signs for the rest of the trip home. His casual observations were uttered with the enthusiasm of a four-year old just learning the words we attach to mundane objects around us. Had Mark not been silent for so long, it may have become a festering annoyance, but considering the circumstances, it was instead a heart-warming twist. Susan flipped down the sun visor revealing the mirror to feign looking at her eye shadow while glancing back to Mark, locked into the wheelchair mount, glowing with happiness for the first time since November. A small tear balled up in the corner of her tired eye and dripped down the side of her cheek as she let out a long sigh of relief.

The turn signal click-clacked for the last time before turning onto Sycamore Court. The car took the familiar straight path up the driveway directly perpendicular to the cross-street. Up the little bump, and through the slowly opening garage door.

"Home at last," Mark said, still high on the ability to think something and allow the speaker to echo his words and vocal reflections.

Ӂ

In his wheelchair, Mark was trapped on the first floor between the basement, which was formerly finished as his childhood playroom, and the upstairs where his old bedroom beckoned. He now resided in the office where his parents used to hold their budgeting meetings and pay the bills. His immediacy for a first floor room caused the contents of the office to be haphazardly scattered to the far corners of the rest of the downstairs, but in the last six months the family stress had been too high to prioritize permanent relocation of the old office artifacts. The desk was now awkwardly wedged beside the leather corner couch in such a manner one could not be on the computer and watch television at the same time. The old letter holder with the incoming and outgoing bills now took up residence in the kitchen by the refrigerator, while the old files and family medical records remained in their off-white metal filing cabinet in the old office. Now it also sported a lamp in Mark's makeshift bedroom.

His new room was more utilitarian than pleasurable. He had a bed he could not lay on at will, and a table where he could roll his chair up to, but not use. He rolled to that table sometimes to think, but he was sick of thinking; he longed to actually be able to do something. His childhood dresser remained upstairs while a cheap particle board big-box special held his necessary seasonal clothes. While he used to treasure time in his upstairs room tinkering with mechanical arms and software commands, he now sought opportunities to flee his new sterile room. His new solace was the back porch, which used to mean little to him, but now provided his favorite thinking spot. It was just outside his door, through the dinning room, into the kitchen, and out the patio door, which was controlled by a newly installed push-button motor allowing Mark to easily enter and exit the kitchen without anyone's aid. That was about the extent of his freedoms and the ability to open and close this door for himself was secretly his reason for liking the back patio so much.

"Cuckoo, Cuckoo, Cuckoo, Cuckoo," the clock reminded everyone that Kristy and Sam would be over in about an hour. His sister, eager to know the result of the operation, was coming over for dinner. Susan was in the kitchen preparing a cornucopia of foods which Mark could not eat. It smelled like Salmon, baked with rosemary and other spices. This was Mark and Kristy's favorite meal as kids, so he surmised a lightly salted broccoli covered in cheddar cheese as the side dish. He let out a small sigh of dejection as it suddenly came to his remembrance that his dinner would be something ground into a baby food consistency or sucked through a straw. He longed to just roll into the kitchen to ask what was for dinner for the first time since November, but he already knew the answer and did not want to think about it anymore.

3

"Ding dong din don…Ding Dong DIN DON" the doorbell rang, announcing Kristy's arrival. The front door was locked or her hands were full; either way she needed the door opened. Mark never flinched from his place in front of the television because he was unable to open the door anyway, but he did muster the mighty strength needed to push the off button on the television remote which Eric had placed under his scrawny fingers by his wheelchair controls. He had worked hard with a physical therapist to be able to push simple buttons to move about in the wheelchair, dominate the television remote, and open the patio door, but life with a single finger is generally quite unfulfilling.

Susan appeared from the kitchen walking past Mark to spin the lock on the front door and swing it open.

"How are you, honey?" Susan asked, embracing Kristy, who was not hugging back because of the two bags still in her hands. Just at that moment, Sam squeezed through the front screen door behind his wife with a little bundle of joy in his arms. Almost ignoring him, Susan went right for the baby, "And how's little Emily?"

"Wet!" Sam retorted.

"Hello," The speaker announced from the basket on the wheelchair behind Mark's head.

Kristy and Sam gazed toward him in astonishment. They were expecting some progress to Mark's condition from the earlier discussions about the implant, but they did not anticipate a full range of vocal communications the day he arrived home from the hospital.

Sam passed Emily to Susan, still fixing his eyes on his brother-in-law. He walked toward him looking just over Mark's head to the speaker laying in the basket on the back of the chair.

"Does that thing think for you?"

"No, I do the thinking, it just does the talking for me."

"That's incredible!"

"More than the Hulk," Mark replied, half excited and half depressed.

Kristy bent down, her hair falling in Mark's face, as she awkwardly embraced him through the wheelchair.

"So, we can actually have conversations again?" she inquired.

"Yes. It will not be my old voice, but at least it does not sound like that terrible voice synthesizer. And it is not as difficult to use either."

"Ever accidentally say something you didn't mean to?"

Mark tested this very question while alone in the hospital. It is difficult to express in words, but we, who are able to speak, or at least have been able to in the past, know the difference between talking and thinking about something. We know what we want to say as compared to what we actually do say. Mark's speaker could tell the difference between what he was thinking and what he was trying to say, and only what he wanted to say was deployed.

Mark used the opportunity to joke around with his sister for the first time in too long. He spit out, "That dress is ugly!"

Kristy fixed on his eyes and backed up an inch, and then looked down on her favorite dress she saved for this occasion.

"Yep, it seems to say what I am thinking! Ha, ha, ha!" Mark said after a pause.

"You're just glad I don't have a speaker to say what I'm thinking!" she countered.

"But it's incredible we can actually talk to each other now." She continued.

"DING!"

The unmistakable sound of the kitchen timer summoned Susan to check on dinner. She passed Emily back to Sam and walked out of the living room into the kitchen and was heard by the rest of them fiddling with spoons and pots.

Ӂ

Dinner was served and the conversation turned to Mark and the new implant.

"So, what's this thing do anyway? Your parents couldn't explain it to us." Sam asked.

The implant was a test protocol and Mark was Patient Zero. By circumstance of his career goals he happened to know the right people at the right time to be introduced to the new company, Synaptergy, which produced the device. It was simple in design containing an RF frequency field providing a proximity login for automatic door locks and computer systems based on the unique ID of the chip, but it also contained a new technology similar to our well known Bluetooth, but more secure, if not by protocol, than by obscurity.

"Well, it is a little complicated." Mark replied while sucking down some thinned apple sauce through a straw, "It wraps itself around the synapses of the brain cells and collects the signals I attempt to send to my limbs. We can capture the signals and map them to functions in a program that will actually do the work. It is sort of like programming a universal TV remote. The device sends out a lot of signals, we just have to map those signals to the right device to control them."

"So you can talk just by thinking, but could you do more?" Sam asked.

Part of Mark wanted to just spit out the plans they had for the implant, but he also did not want to raise false hopes with his family. Rather than expounding on his dreams of once again walking or taking care of himself, he chose instead to take a conservative approach.

"We pretty much knew the talking would work, so we were confident about that, but as for the rest, we can only guess. Hopefully we will be able to collect signals and figure out what's supposed to go to a finger or toe or arm or leg and program a computer to do what we are trying to do with our head, but I am not sure if we can even do that. Talking is a good start!"

"Do you think you'd ever be able to walk with it?"

The questions were still trying to get Mark to talk about what he did not want to consider right now. He tempered his thoughts instead, providing a more coy response, "Well, I am not sure. We will know more when we start doing the tests.

Kristy looked up from her salmon patty, "Who's doing the tests?"

"Our tests are actually going to be done in my old lab. Synaptergy funded the whole initiative and Professor David was appointed the principal investigator for the project at large. As both a student in the lab and Patient Zero, I get to help with the protocols. As for the tests themselves, I have to think about wanting to walk, or move my arm, or something else like that, and we will be collecting those signals and figuring out how to map them to robotic commands."

"When will the doctors let you start?"

"I'll answer that," Eric interjected, "This type of surgery is very new but is supposed to be the safest type of surgery. A laser was used to cut exactly what was needed but it also prevents any bleeding. In reality, after only a day or two he should be able to do the work, but since it is a new surgery method, they will wait two weeks and do some CT scans to make sure everything's fine."

While Eric was giving his explanation of the medical procedure, Kristy filled Emily's mouth with baby food while Susan stuffed some similar concoction into Mark's mouth. He looked to his niece who was accepting her dinner with surprisingly less difficulty than he was. He muscled down the soft food to not be outdone by the infant in the room. While he still had the spoon in his mouth, the speaker added,

"But Dad will let me start early!"

Kristy, observing the spoon in his mouth while talking, joked, "Don't talk with your mouth full!"

Everyone had a chuckle over this, but then Eric piped back up. "I think you should spend the next few weeks learning the limits of the speaker so you'll know for sure how to best communicate when you're back in the lab."

This was the most animated anyone had seen Mark since November. Even though he still did not have the use of his limbs, the implant gave him back communication, propelling Mark back into research mode and giving him the promise of restoring some of his former life.

4

"How's the work going, Sam?" Eric inquired as he sank into his usual place on the far left of the couch, nearly opposite the television. With typical male intrigue, the two men started all conversations at the surface level pleasantries of work. Not that deeper matters were off the list, but for some reason they always started every visit exactly the same way.

"Not too bad," came his predictable answer as he settled just beyond the bend in the couch with Emily snugly in his right arm while holding a bottle in the left. He fixed his blue eyes on his baby, admiring his wife's face in their joint creation.

"We have a few new machines to assemble. I just got the blueprints in this afternoon," he finally said after a pause.

Sam was an assembly manager directing a team of people who assembled circuit boards and other components for robotics manufacturing. He took the job as something to do for the summer just out of high school on the floor of the factory, learning how to gently set tiny chips onto board paste, preparing them to go into the baking oven to solder the chips in place. He decided he liked that kind of work and saw a long-term need for such a company. Instead of quitting to go off to college, he took night courses in business management and was eventually promoted to his current management role. Sam boasted the assembly of such machines as Flippy, the burger flipper and a smoothie making robot for some small California startup company.

"What's this new one do?" Eric asked, squaring his shoulders toward Sam.

"What I understand, and they are not terribly clear about these things until we see them in the news, it'll close down that last lane in the grocery store that's always open because they sell ID-required restricted products by confirming someone's identity before fulfilling an order."

"Like a pack of cigarettes?"

Sam paused for a moment in the conversation setting down the bottle and picking up Emily to place her over his shoulder to induce a belch. He continued, "Yep, or chew, or over-the-counter medicines. Whatever might need an ID to approve the sale."

Focusing his attention on their conversation, Mark turned his wheelchair around. "How does it work? Like, how does it know what to get, or that you should not buy something?"

"Well, I'm not a computer guy, so I don't know the insides, but it has the usual stuff you would expect from a robotic clerk that grabs the merchandise for you; like an old west general store."

Mark longed for the challenge he faced in the old college courses: 'Describe the components of a machine that would sell restricted merchandise.' He thought about how he would answer that as an essay question. First, scan an ID, but the ID needs to verify that it was not stolen, so the customer now needs to look at a camera for a facial scan. Once the ID matches a facial recognition database, the touchscreen activates and provides a list of restricted products available to the ID owner. The robotic arm then grabs the products, charges them to the account on file, and releases the merchandise to the customer.

This, of course, would also keep a record of who bought which restricted items for legal reasons.

After thinking about how he would have answered the question in class, he gave a summarized explanation, "It probably checks and verifies the ID prior to allowing the person to select the products they want and then giving them the choices."

"Hmm…" Sam sounded with a slight nod. "That sounds like it matches the parts list for the schematics! How'd you put that together?"

"Well, we were always asked to describe how we would make specific types of robotics on our essays. I usually did well on those questions."

Right about then, Susan and Kristy walked into the living room, Susan announcing that the dishes were washed, as if everyone in the room was anticipating the news. She excitedly walked to the opposite corner of the living room from where the couch was positioned and rustled through some bags of yarn and patterns, finally pulling out a mini pink sweater. Mark recognized it as the now-completed object she was working on when he woke up in the recovery room.

"Here's the sweater I told you about, Kristy."

Sam handed the baby off to his wife with an oblong smile. Kristy walked the baby to grandma, now holding

Emily near her bottom allowing Susan to slip the sweater over her tiny head.

"Fits perfectly!" She boasted with pride.

Kristy and Sam looked Emily over. The sweater was a hilarious juxtaposition against the white onesie. Their baby now resembled Donald Duck: wearing a shirt but no pants. They smiled at grandma's kind gesture and thanked her for the gift.

"Wawawawa, Wawawawa, Wawawawa," the cellphone on the edge of the desk squealed to announce an incoming call. Susan, standing nearest the phone looked at the contact name, "Wawawawa, wawawawa," the phone continued.

"Mark! It's Professor David! Everyone quiet!" She commanded, answering the phone directly onto speaker.

"Hello Professor!" Mark said.

"Mark?" The voice hesitated, "Is that you?"

"Yep! I can hear you and actually talk on the phone!"

"Incredible!" He yelled with excitement. "And I thought I'd just call to ask your parents how you're doing!"

"I can talk again so this crazy implant must be working. I can not wait to start thinking of new ways to test the chip."

"That's great! The lab is about ready to have you back. Is your Dad around?"

"I'm right here," Eric said, announcing his presence on the phone.

"How long do the doctors at the hospital reckon it will be before he can start doing tests?"

"Well," Eric started, "John, the head of the medical team, liked the results from the initial CT scan after the operation was completed. He wants Mark to have a few weeks of rest before we get into serious work, though."

"But I bet Dad will let me start sooner!" Mark interrupted.

"Maybe," Eric hesitated, "But there's nothing wrong with talking things over and starting a few plans. He can't make it into the lab for at least a week, but you are welcome over any time to start discussing the next steps of the project."

"Is that OK with you, Mark?"

"Please come over! I am soooo bored with watching television!"

"Well, I have something for you, so I think I can make it over between classes tomorrow morning. How about directly after the 11:00 Intro to Robotics?"

"Sound's great. See you then!" Mark exclaimed with excitement.

Susan interrupted this time, "Plan to have some lunch, that is your lunch break, right?"

"Yes, I'll do that. Thank you!"

"OK, we will see you then. Bye!"

"Bye" "Bye!" Eric and Mark inched in before the call disconnected. Susan placed the phone back down on the corner of the desk and settled down next to Eric, wrapping her arm around him. Kristy laid Emily in grandma's free arms and grabbed the television remote from the wheelchair control arm and started looking for a movie to watch as a family.

Ӂ

"We gotta get home," Sam pushed through his yawn, "Early start at the factory tomorrow." He and Kristy gave Mark a final hug and told him he should come over on Saturday like he used to. They gathered their bags of baby gear and walked out the door. Eric saw it closed and firmly turned the deadbolt.

Susan stretched a final time, herself announcing it was way past her bedtime. She and Kristy were the morning people, while Eric and Mark were the night owls of the family.

"Goodnight Mom!" Mark voiced. This was his first goodnight in six months. She firmly hugged Mark in the wheelchair for about twice as long as she had done on prior nights, but she finally eased the embrace and walked down the hall and up the stairs to bed.

"Well," Eric said, "I have a few bills to see to if you don't mind."

"Not at all, Dad. I think I will go outside for a bit."

"OK, but not for too long. It's getting cold."

"Can you put that blanket on me?" referring to the perfectly crafted afghan that was always folded on the back of the couch.

Eric complied, pulling the blanket from the couch and wrapping it around him tucking it under the left arm but casually laying it across his right hand so he could still control the wheelchair.

"Let me know if you need anything." He would have offered to open the patio door, but he knew Mark would deny the help if asked. Eric knew his son wanted as much independence as he could possibly muster, and appreciated that the patio door was about all he could get.

Eric took his seat at the desk a mere few feet from where he always sat on the couch. He opened up the drawer to grab the checkbook just when he heard the patio door open, the wheelchair roll out, and then close again.

It was a typical April night, a little cool, but clear. Mark slowly moved his head up to glance at the stars. He could make out the eternal battle between Orion and Taurus from his usual thinking spot just outside the patio door. He sighed and reflected back to the events of the day: waking up able to talk, engaging in casual conversations. Yes, Mark was so happy to be able to have discourse again.

A short 'what if' panic entered his mind. What if he had never studied anything about robotics? What if he never met Professor David? What would have happened to him if he found himself in this state and did not have the opportunity to meet the people at Synaptergy? A tear rolled down his face while he mourned the loss of the use of his body, but it was tempered with the opportunity to see technology restore his most prized asset: to talk with his family again. His head nodded down a bit in exhaustion, but he was instantly jolted awake by mechanical sliding of the patio door.

"Come on in now, Mark."

"OK," he said, turning his chair and aligning it with the small ramp. He rolled in, through the kitchen and started moving through the dining room.

"Mark..." Eric said softly.

The chair stopped, but did not turn, "What?"

"Well, since you can talk now, I thought we might stay up a bit like we used to."

The chair slowly turned, "I would like nothing more, Dad."

The electric teapot in the kitchen began a low rumbling boil. Eric knew the answer his son would give and started the water on before opening the door. Dad flipped up the switch to turn off the pot and grabbed two mugs. Reaching for the container of hot chocolate, he burst into tears instead. He backed away from the familiar Swiss Miss canister and made a quarter turn to Mark. They both knew the problem as Mark looked down. The last time father and son shared hot chocolate from that very canister was a cold November night. The same last night either parents had ever heard his real voice. While dad was in tears, Mark was somber, but not teary. He broke the silence.

"Dad, there was nothing you could do. Let us just move on."

"But what if I could've done more?" He sniffled, plucking up the hot chocolate canister as if speed was of the essence. He carried the fated container to the table for the first time in six months. After filling the cups with hot water, he brought them to the table with shaking hands. One more trip was needed to the kitchen to grab a spoon and Mark's straw from the dish washer. Meanwhile, Mark rolled into his usual spot at the dining room table: the unmistakable one with the place-mat but no chair. Eric started shoveling heaping spoonfuls of mix into each cup and stirred them sequentially with the spoon. He finally dropped the long straw into one of the cups and slid it over in front of Mark.

There was an unusual silence between father and son, at least unusual compared to their many past conversations about life, education, girls, and even *The Talk*. Their last six months, however, held very little communication. For Mark's part, speaking was a belabored task, taking between fifteen and thirty seconds to manufacture a sentence on ACAT. But while Mark was unable to talk, Eric, it seemed, did not really want to. He and Susan had a fight about this a few months back. It was as if she thought they could continue their conversations like nothing had ever happened. Eric, of course, defending himself by suggesting there was a lot on his mind. But no one was privy to the weighty matters bogging him down.

After a few careful slurps with the straw, and while Eric was sipping his cup, Mark finally broke the silence. "I can not wait to get back to the lab."

"In due time, Mark."

The answer was a little unusual. In the past, Eric always supported, even encouraged, fast progress, even with a hint of recklessness. Conversations of the past would be more inquisitive and open-ended. He would have asked what his first idea was, how it might be tested. It was that old desire for research his father had in his heart.

"Do you know what I want to do first?"

"What?" Eric said while his cup was in front of his mouth.

"Is something wrong, Dad?" Mark changed the subject.

The cup softly hit the table and a quick smile hit his face in the way Mark knew it was a forced reaction to his question. "I'm fine!" He exclaimed, "Just tired."

Mark knew it was a farce, but chose to ignore the reaction. He just longed for a conversation much like they used to have, even if both parties did not have their heart fully invested.

"First I want to think about walking and see what types of signals the implant releases. Then we might be able to make something like a foot to see if we can duplicate the way a real foot moves."

This started the wheels churning in Eric's mind. For the first time tonight, he seemed interested in the conversation.

"You might need to create little components for every muscle and tendon in the leg if you want to try that. It'd be rather difficult."

"Yep. Can you help with the basic parts of the leg? We will try the major muscles first and then add in the small ones as needed."

"I can help with that part...put those old anatomy courses to good use!" After a pause, he continued, "How'll you be collecting these signals?"

"We have a computer at the lab that can read everything the chip is sending out. It records the raw data, so we need to figure out what they all do by reading the signals while resting and thinking of nothing, and then comparing those signals to those emitted when I attempt to do certain tasks like walking or picking up a cup."

"beep...beep...beep..."

"What is that?" Mark asked rolling his head and eyes around.

"Sounded like it was coming from you! Do you beep now?" Eric joked. He stood up and looked at the speaker in the wheelchair basket. The black frame contained only a couple little buttons which neither of them knew what they did. It had a large speaker, and a flashing red light which seemed to indicate the battery was low.

"Well, it looks like it's your speaker's bedtime!" he said in the way he might address a defiant toddler resisting his nightly sleep.

Mark sucked down the rest of the hot chocolate causing a final rough slurp with his straw. Eric likewise threw back the last gulp of his drink, grabbed both cups and walked them to the sink, filling the cups with water to soak for the night.

Mark rolled back to his bedroom where Eric lifted him out of his chair and placed him into bed and tucked him in. The wheelchair was plugged into the charging dock and the speaker likewise plugged into the wall but was placed on the nightstand next to the bed.

"Good night."

5

It must have been shortly after nine in the morning when the sun peaked over the treeline and into the window illuminating Mark's face. He woke up to the rude, bright sun shining into his eyes. The daily ritual was about to begin. He would ordinarily use a buzzer positioned on his bed to call through the house for aid, but he heard Mom's distinctive cough-clear near by in the living room.

"Mom!" The speaker yelled out.

A brief rustle of crochet patterns was heard, then a moment later Susan was in the room.

"Time to get up," which was Mark's code word for saying, "I need to use the bathroom," without actually saying those humiliating words.

Mark did have control over those natural functions, but also wore washable diapers in the event he was unable to get help in the bathroom. The ritual began as Mark was set in a frame in the first level bathroom being robbed of his lower garments. It was his daily humiliation: his mother set the nearly naked seventeen year old body on the toilet. He would relieve himself and then call for the next steps before being bathed and dressed. The whole ritual usually took about forty-five minutes, and Mark was counting the time until Professor David would arrive.

Susan finished the morning wake up ritual, secured Mark into the chair, and moved the speaker back to the basket. It was time for the next humiliating part of the day: breakfast.

Mark took up his spot at the table, "What is in the blender today?" Not that the answer mattered. Once a meal is blended, the tastes change around, but one loses the appreciation for food due to the loss of texture.

"Today we are having your favorite: fruit smoothie." Mark did enjoy the smoothies. Susan perfected the home made mix with berries and banana, yogurt frozen into cubes, milk, and ice. Once blended together, the smoothie was actually very filling and nutritious. She added, "I didn't want you to start the first day of being able to talk to me whining about horrible food."

She was half serious because Mark was never pleased with his dietary options these days, but she was also joking, wanting to give him the best, first full day being able to communicate.

"This is particularly good today," he complimented. Not that it was any better than usual, but it was not baby food, and he could actually compliment the chef without labor for the first time. He finished the drink, said thank you, and rolled back into the bedroom.

"Do you want the television on?" Mom called, still rinsing dishes to fill the dishwasher.

"No."

His usual morning would be spent wasting away in front of the television, but today, ideas where on his mind. Of course, he also had the problem of what to do with them. He could talk, yet he had no way of writing down the brainstorming sessions flashing through his mind. Perhaps a nap was in order, so he sank his head into the cushion on the back of his chair and closed his eyes.

Ӂ

"This is Mark," the professor said to the class of students about four years older than Mark.

"While he's younger that you guys, still a...what year are you in?"

"I'm a junior," Mark completed.

"While he's still a junior in high school, he's quite knowledgeable in the field already. In fact, he has been tinkering around with robotics since he was a kid and takes his education very seriously. I expect you all to welcome him into this class."

After the introduction, Mark sat down in the empty chair, third row from the window. He looked around the room gathering context clues for the proper college conduct. He deduced the protocol in this class was sliding his book bag under the chair which he did before nervously realizing he needed a notebook, so he retrieved the bag again from beneath his chair and slowly unzipped it as too not draw attention. Of course, all students know that the harder one tries to silence a zipper, the more noise it actually makes. Mark could feel the eyes training on him, but he nevertheless extracted the notebook and quietly slid the bag back under the chair while looking around to see if anyone was watching him. Now he was ready.

"Hi!" A large black hand appeared in front of his face while he straightened up from sliding his bag under the chair. "I'm Micheal," the boy continued.

Mark grabbed his hand, which felt like he was arm wrestling a football player. "Nice to meet you," he courteously replied.

"Is this your first day?"

"Yep. It's a lot bigger than high school around here," he chuckled nervously.

"Yeah, but you'll get used to it. If anyone gives you trouble, just let me know!"

"Thanks," Mark replied with a smile. "Is Professor David a good teacher?"

"I've not had him yet, but my friend in the dorms really learned a lot in this class last year. Prof is tough, but apparently teaches well."

Mark's first day of class was actually not the first time he had met Professor David. They first met when he was one of a dozen thirteen-year old kids descending on campus for a summer robotics camp sponsored by the university. Mark did not know as much then and would not have stood out as an extraordinary student, but the professor's expertise showed Mark exactly what he wanted to do with his life, and thus impacted his goals. He had worked hard and used up his electives and required projects in high school to be able to take the advanced courses and be admitted into the university, which would also allow him to graduate high school with an associates degree as well as a high school diploma. Such a plan also guaranteed him a seat at the local university and possibly a position in a lab.

The semester carried on and Mark showed to be a competent student on level with the rest of his classmates. He was neither so advanced in the field as to be bored, nor seen as a know-it-all, but he also did not struggle. He met with other students for study groups, gave and received reciprocal help, and contributed to his lab group appropriately. He became well liked, not for his youth, nor achievements, but because he seemed to fit in with the rest of his classmates astonishingly well. Mostly, he formed a great friendship with Micheal who would also be his lab partner for the next two semesters of robotics courses.

Mark's primary motivation was his desire to spend more time with Professor David. He knew robotics were his future and having a mentor would help him in both education and possible future connections. Mark did his best in the classroom studies, but he also tried hard to excel in the labs, which for Mark was not class. It was an extension of his childhood, but with real world applications.

Over the course of the semester, the professor took an interest in Mark because of his dedication. A lot of students can achieve the grades, and most will try their best, but there was something David saw in Mark that caused him to take special notice. It was not the academics, nor his youth. Mark also was not a specifically gifted young man, but he exhibited a drive to succeed. It was the basis of his drive that caused the professor to ask him to stay after class near the end of the semester.

"You wanted to see me, professor?"

"Yes, Mark. Thanks for staying after. I'll get right to the point. I have been watching your dedication to robotics, and I see something that is not just competence or a desire for a job. I see a person who wants to go above and beyond in this field. On that basis, I want to ask you if you're interested in joining the lab. It is not a paid position, but it does satisfy all research requirements and it will continue to apply to all research credits until you have finished all the degrees you want. We can also pick up most of your education costs. Talk it over with your parents and see what they have to say. If you're on board, and they're on board, let's schedule a meeting and get started right after the Christmas break."

Mark busted out in the biggest smile he ever made, but he also tried to hold it back. "I'm very interested…and I think my parents will be fine with it…"

Professor David cut him off there. "You do not have to hide your excitement, Mark. You've earned this. Talk it over with your parents, and we will talk about all the requirements in the meeting."

Ж

Mark jolted awake, looking toward the desk in his room. His computer was brought down into the room, though had not been powered on in a long time. The hard drive held all the assignments he had completed for his first college level robotics courses. The sight of the computer gave him the flashback of his first semester that started only eighteen months ago, though it seemed like an eternity now.

He examined the tower looking at the USB and SD card ports and CD tray on the front. Wires jetted out of the back of the black computer case like some dead sea creature. The dust collecting on the computer bothered him, but there wasn't anything he could do about it. He glanced over at the clock to see the time: just past 11:30. He tried with all his effort to make a smile appear on his face, and he made his way to the living room, anticipating David's arrival.

"Ding dong din don...Ding Dong DIN DON."

"Mom! GET THE DOOR!" he shouted with the speaker emitting sound louder than usual.

"I'm coming!" She yelled from her position at the upstairs banister.

Mark, unable to contain his excitement, positioned his chair to look out the window. Seeing movement just inside, Professor David smiled and waved. Susan arrived at the living room and opened the door.

"Come on in, professor!" She said while swinging the door open.

"Please, call me David," he reminded, as he always did. But she had a regular habit of calling him professor because that's what Mark always referred to him as.

"I got something for you," now addressing Mark. He lifted a small cup with that familiar golden M on the side. Yes, the one delight that could not be changed even by the events six months ago: Mark had a love for chocolate milkshakes.

"Thanks," he said, now happy both for the shake and the ability to easily voice his gratitude. The professor placed the shake in the drink holder on the side of the chair near his head.

"You guys make yourselves comfortable," Susan said, now in the dining room rustling through the drawer. She emerged back into the living room bringing the thick bent straw and placing it into the milkshake, positioning it for Mark to sip at will.

"Well," the professor said taking the same seat on the couch that Sam had the night before. "I brought you more than a milkshake."

"What is it?"

"Just this," The professor pulled a small device out of his front shirt pocket. Mark recognized it immediately as a USB device of sorts. It was small, like a receiver for a mouse or keyboard, or maybe a Bluetooth chip.

"What is it?" Mark repeated, now knowing that it was a computer component, but still unsure of the significance.

"It's a little gift from Tyler. This receiver will accept the signals to control HIDs on the computer, so you should be able to use the computer just by thinking about it."

"HIDs?" Susan asked from Eric's chair at the desk.

"Human Input Devices...like a keyboard or mouse," The professor answered.

Mark turned his chair toward the doorway, "Let us go set it up!"

He led the way past his mom who smiled, announcing she would start lunch.

Mark led the professor to the bedroom where the computer was sitting idle on the desk. Upon seeing the layer of dust, he wiped his hand across the top and blew the dust into the air behind him.

"Yep, it has gotten dusty. I should have asked someone to clean it up a while ago, but I have had too much on my mind."

"That's fine, but do get it cleaned up when you can. Treat the equipment well and it'll last a long time." he scolded with a teacher's instructive tone.

David pressed the power button and the soft sounds of booting hardware rumbled and the fans started to spin, spewing out a small collection of dust. The login screen proudly displayed 'Debian' while waiting for the username and password. Mark told David the credentials and the desktop booted up quickly.

David plugged the USB receiver into the back of the computer and pulled a flash drive out of his pocket.

"'Got the drivers right here." he announced, plugging in the device into a rear port. David booted up a terminal, mounted the drive, and navigated to a bash script for driver setup.

The installation took about three minutes, but to Mark, it seemed like an eternity. Once the script had run its course and the bash prompt awaited another input, the system rebooted. The login screen again displayed, and David instructed Mark to give it a try.

"How?" he asked.

"I'm not really sure. Maybe think about the process you might use to login, like see what'd happen if you tried to move your hands over the keyboard."

Mark thought for a moment and tried in vain to move his arm. Then he just thought about the process he might use to type into the keyboard. All of a sudden, as if by magic, "m-a-r-k" displayed on the screen. The cursor jumped to the password field followed by "*-*-*-*-*-*-*-*-*-*" and the system landed on the desktop.

They both let out a gasp as though they were half expecting the receiver to do nothing, but it completed its task flawlessly.

"How'd you do it?"

"I am not sure. It is kind of like talking with the speaker, I just 'know' how to talk. I always knew how to talk and knew how to walk, and knew the difference between thinking my password and actively typing it. The words just appeared as I thought them."

Mark controlled the mouse with the same results. A mere thought scrolled the mouse across the screen and up to the left corner displaying the application launcher. He jumped quickly down to the Atom text editor and booted up the application and within a few seconds, he started spitting out words on the document. He was able to type as fast as a person can think, which is much faster than manually hitting keys, and more efficient than clunky speech to text applications.

"If only I had this when I needed to write your term papers, I could have finished in half the time!" he chuckled to the professor.

"Well, so much for assigning busy work," he countered with a joking tone.

Mark was testing the speed he could launch applications, type down lists, and even do basic coding.

He found excitement once again using his computer, now even better than he had in the past. In a way, he wished he was always able to just think about what he wanted and see it happen.

"Lunch is ready," Susan interrupted. She had been standing in the door for about a minute just watching. Once she spoke up, David turned around in surprise.

"Look at this, Mom," Mark said in a moment. She walked to the screen examining what they were looking at, half expecting some funny video or a game or something uninteresting. Susan was not able to program the DVR, and she touched computers as seldom as possible. Peering at the screen, she had no idea what she was looking at.

"What is so interesting?" she asked.

Just then, Mark guided his thoughts to open Atom. Words suddenly appeared on the screen:

I AM TYPING THIS WITH MY MIND

"Huh," she said with a somewhat concerning voice. "Let's go eat." she finally said as if trying to change the focus. Professor David walked out of the room followed by Mark. Susan took a final look at the screen, sighed, and followed the other two out.

ж

Mark rolled to his position at the table but David stood in the dining area looking back to Susan who was just leaving the room and approaching the dining room.

"Need any help?" He asked.

"No, you just have a seat," she said passing both of them, heading beyond the divider wall into the kitchen, emerging a moment later with a sandwich on a white plate for the professor and some blended strained squash for Mark. She handed the sandwich to the professor and placed the squash in a bowl on the place-mat in front of Mark. Her own sandwich and some water for the professor was retrieved from the kitchen and she finally sat down at the table opposite David in the seat next to Mark.

"Do I need to eat now? I'm not hungry," he protested. In reality, he was actually quite starving but did not like to be fed in front of his friend. Had he started the day with the squash and had the smoothie now, he would have been happier.

"You need to eat now, Mark." She barked, picking up a spoonful of mush.

Mark did not protest because he wanted to display maturity in front of Professor David. Eating would not stop his conversation about the use of the computer.

"Now that the computer works, I can start writing down my ideas for when we get back to the lab," Mark said excitedly.

"Well, let me know of anything you might need, and we'll get it all setup before you make it back. We almost have your new desk assembled. I still need to get the second receiver from Tyler for your lab computer, but I'll see him tomorrow, so I might get it then."

"I still need to get the Internet connected to my computer. The wire does not reach over to where the computer sits. Can we get to that today, mom?"

"Your dad does not want you to start back in on research yet, Mark, so let's just wait a few weeks before you connect to the world."

"But, Mom, I can get computer work done. Dad did not say I could not do that!" But he was not winning his case.

"No, Mark, I don't want to connect your computer to the Internet just yet...So, David, how's the class going?" Susan said, changing the subject rather than continue the fight.

"Not too bad. This is the last couple weeks before finals, so we're wrapping up the new material and starting the reviews and exam preparations."

"Do you still have the lab final where the students need to build the arm and install the software?" Mark interjected.

"Yes. That worked well for the last few years I've been trying it, so we're going to stick with it."

David paused, sliding the last of the baloney sandwich into his mouth and washing it down with some water.

"Did you get enough to eat?" Susan asked while David was grabbing a handful of chips from the bowl in the center of the table.

"Yes, plenty, thank you," He glanced down at his watch, "Well, it looks like the 2:00 class will be starting soon, so I need to get back."

"Thanks for staying for lunch, David," Susan said, scraping the last bit of squash into the spoon. She slid it into Mark's mouth and followed with the towel to clean off his face.

"I will see you out," Mark backed away from the table and spun toward the door. "Do you have the software we need to start collecting the signals from the implant?" He asked en route to the front door.

"Not yet, Mark. That is something I'm going to talk with Tyler about when I see him tomorrow."

"Let me know as soon as you have it. I want to see how it works."

"I will," and with that, Professor David closed the door behind him and walked back to his car.

Mark watched through the window as the silver Honda turned left at the end of the street. Once he could no longer see the car, he turned around and made the way back into his room to work on the computer some more.

6

Mark was already accessing the application menu, scrolling to the last page of programs before he fully rolled in front of the computer. Once positioned to see the screen, the word processor opened up and Mark was already titling the writer document and saving a copy of the blank page minus the header.

"TO DO:" displayed on the screen followed by a blinking cursor.

Mark started typing a list of random items with his mind.

"Eat"

"Use the bathroom alone"

"Walk"

"Move my hands"

"Dress myself"

He admired the list, thinking about the order they should appear. His priority should be to regain the use of his arms and hands. If he could do that, he reasoned, most of the list should be manageable. Even if he could not figure out how to chew food, at least controlling when he took a bite would be helpful for regaining much of his lost dignity. Also, if he had arm control, he could use railings in the bathroom even without being able to walk.

"Move my arms and hands"

"Use the bathroom and eat"

"Walk"

He finally settled on the order.

"HOW," he wrote in the header for a new section.

Mark paused, thinking about how to gain the use of his hands. Glancing down on those hands, he realized he always took them for granted. They lied lifelessly attached to his body, but completely unusable. They had atrophied to the bone by the inability to move them over the last six months. While Mark had never been a performance athlete, he had also not looked so scrawny since he was the thirteen-year-old boy who first attended robotics camp.

"Implants"

"Exoskeleton"

"Robot assistant"

"Cyborg arm"

"Nah, too creepy," he thought to himself as he typed that last item. But still, for completion, he wanted to keep it on the list, so a he applied a strike through: "~~Cyborg arm~~".

"No one would actually take this item seriously, would they?" He said to himself, but he also wanted to make sure they knew it had crossed his mind.

Admiring his list, he decided that implants should also be low on the list and a robotic assistant would be the perfect test case project with an exoskeleton as the ultimate goal.

He saved the file in his folder for projects and launched a new document.

"ROBOT ASSISTANT," appeared as the title of the new document.

He gave pause to think about the tasks needed to accomplish this project:

> To create a robotic assistant that can be controlled with the implant to do basic tasks such as grab objects, open doors and windows, pick up dropped items.

"PARTS" was listed under the introductory paragraph. His coursework on how to set up a project was coming back to him.

"Implant interface software"

"Raspberry Pi"

"Robotics components"

"Power supply"

The document was saved and Mark pulled up a PDF with Raspberry Pi specs. He was admiring the board diagram thinking about which switch feeds could control the various components. He was jarred out of his concentration by the loud thud of the kitchen door.

"Hello!" He heard his dad call out. It must have been about 5:30, the usual time Eric came in from work.

"Hi honey!" Susan said from upstairs, "How was your day?" She started walking down the stairs which landed just in front of Mark's door. She peeked into his room and walked across the dining room to where Eric was dropping keys in the bowl reserved for important items.

"Just fine," he casually remarked, "No major operations today, just some scraped knees and a minor bike crash. Where's Mark?" He added to his list of medical procedures of the day.

"In his room," was all Mark heard audibly. Susan said something else that seemed intentionally quiet and muffled. He heard the low "Ah Huhs" and "OKs" of a secret conversation and then his father went into Mark's room making considerably more noise.

"What's going on Mark?"

"Look at this dad. I can use the computer again!" He exclaimed, now looking up from the circuit diagrams on the computer screen.

"That's cool. You will have to show me how it works later, but for now, we think you should come out for a bit."

Mark instantly realized that the soft tones were expressed dissatisfaction to the amount of time Mark was on the computer, though the concern was not directed his way. He did not even care if it was. All Mark could think of was his exuberance of being able to do something remotely productive; the instant regaining of somewhat functional life.

"If I have to," he said disinterestedly.

"Yes, you do. We're going to go out for some air."

Mark did enjoy going outside for the family walks which usually occurred between the time Eric made it home and dinner which was usually closer to 7:00 these days.

Ж

The family always left from the garage door and walked down the cul-de-sac to the end of Sycamore street. The typical walk took the right-hand turn onto Pineview and down about a quarter of a mile to the park which had a concrete walking trail perfect for Mark's wheelchair.

"How's the professor?" Eric asked as they were approaching the stop sign at the end of the street.

"He is fine." Mark answered. "He got the receiver chip to control the computer with the implant, and we installed it, so I can start working on the computer again."

"That's pretty good, Mark, but remember, I don't want you doing work until we get the CT scan results in a few weeks."

"A few word documents of ideas is all I am doing. Can I at least do that?" He shot back. His eyes glanced to the edge of the park concrete sidewalk focusing on a small patch of hedge garlic that was starting to show its white flowers.

"I guess, but I don't want you on the computer all day. There is a time for work and a time for rest."

"Dad, my last six months has been nothing *but* rest! I can not do anything but sit in front of the television. Remember when you did not want me in front of the TV all day? Now that is all I can do!"

"We'll talk about it later, Mark." Susan interjected.

"I want to talk about it now!" Mark yelled back, the speaker becoming louder with agitation.

"Two hours a day, Mark," his father said softly, trying to turn the tone back down.

Mark sighed in frustration. He was so tired of just 'resting' and wanted to put his mind to work solving the conditions afflicting his body. He desperately wanted to continue negotiating, letting them know this was not work, but trying to solve his life dilemma. Mark's greater purpose in his studies and research took over his mind as he struggled with how to become independent again. He was trying to solve not only his problems, but those of people like him. He resented the time limits, but he did not want to draw more attention to it.

"How was work, Dad?" Mark changed the subject, pretending he had heard nothing of the skinned knees earlier.

"Just fine. No deaths, dismemberment, or other crises to handle, just the basic spring time injuries."

"Did you talk to John, today?"

"About what?"

Mark was trying not to place too much attention in wanting doctor's clearance early, but he was also trying to push for an earlier evaluation.

"Anything?" He asked casually to avoid tipping his hand.

"Well, we talked about the dinner at his house on Saturday. I told him we would be attending. I hope that's OK with you, honey." He directed to his wife.

"Who'll take care of Mark?"

"I will be fine, mom."

"I'm not sure I want to leave him alone, Eric." Susan said.

"We won't be leaving him alone. Kristy and Sam already asked him to come over Saturday anyway, so we'll just take Mark over there early so they can have dinner and a movie, and we'll go to the party. Maybe you can just stay overnight there, Mark," directing attention again to his son.

"I guess that is OK." he said.

Susan was equally ambivalent in her reply, and so, the Saturday plans were settled.

"And how was your day?" Eric finally said to Susan.

"Fine. I did the usual, woke up Mark and got him ready for Professor David to come over, made lunch and worked on an afghan for Emily. I also called about the insurance bill. They will not cover the implant surgery because it's experimental."

"I think the lab will be paying that as part of the research. I will ask Professor David." Mark replied.

"Dad and I'll handle this, Mark. You don't need to worry about it."

"Mom, this is part of the research. I have some knowledge on these things!"

"This is your health, Mark, and that's our business," Susan retorted.

For the second time on this walk, Mark was getting frustrated by the insistence that he was not able to contribute in the few ways he was actually able. He looked to the black oak trees on the edge of the park, but turned around before reaching them.

"I am tired and want to go home now." Mark lied after a few minutes of silence between the three of them. He actually wanted to stay outside longer, but his frustration was getting to the best of him, so he longed for time to be alone.

"Alright, if you really want to." Eric said, trying not to sound flustered by the cross words on this walk, but still releasing more emotion with his words than he intended. They turned around and walked back to the house, mostly in silence.

Ӂ

Eric cooled his frustration by checking on the bills at the desk by the couch while Susan was caught in a flurry of activity in the kitchen assembling dinner. It smelled like steak and potatoes, making Mark long for real food. The smell was accompanied by sizzling onions and spice shakers adding just the perfect seasoning he would never taste again. Mark was listening from his room where the computer application menu was again open. He booted the Atom Text Editor and started by adding some comments.

"#Implant Input"

"#If call special movement"

"#If call arm movement"

The code helps were intermingled with sub comments to identify some basic function. Mark knew it was better to execute each of these when the final project was broken into code snippets, but he favored the idea of a single document to start with the brainstorming, and then he would split that code representative parts as each section developed.

Just when he was getting into more explanatory comments, the loud buzz of the blender knocked him out of the zone. While he could still smell the glorious, sizzling cow, he immediately thought about what horrible mush awaited him for his mealtime. He brooded over the loss of his jaw, but all the same, his mouth watered with the thoughts and memories of steak and potatoes.

"Dinner's almost ready!" Susan shouted from the kitchen in such a way to get everyone's attention and summon them to the kitchen for orders. Mark only had one standing order: roll into position at the place-mat without a chair.

Eric closed the drawer in the desk, walked past Mark, and stepped into the kitchen.

"What can I do?" He said disinterestedly, more announcing his presence than looking for orders.

"Get the drinks, please." She ordered anyway.

He grabbed three glasses, filled them with water, and brought them to the table, distributing them to the usual places. He finally went to the cabinet in the dining room to fish out Mark's straw.

Susan entered the room with two plates placing them down on the table before retreating back to the kitchen. Mark stared at the glorious chunk of beef and the steaming potatoes, dreaming of jumping into that plate with fork in hand. This fantasy ended as soon as it began when Susan emerged from the kitchen with a steaming bowl of mush. She sat down at her usual spot next to Mark and stirred the bowl a few times before placing a heap of pureed slop onto the spoon. Mark did not ask what it was; he didn't care.

As the pre-fabricated bolus was ready to for swallowing, Mark realized his dinner was the same steak and potatoes but blended with milk to turn the once glorious meat patty into a baby food consistency. These meals sucked all the pleasure out of eating and gave a whole new dimension to the typical protests of a child who does not like his food to touch. However, Mark could confirm with parents around the world that, indeed, all food goes to the same place.

"What'cha you working on?" Eric asked as the first question to the dinner conversation.

"I am laying out the comments in a program for using the implant to control a robotic arm."

"Dad doesn't want you working, honey." Susan interrupted.

"A few lines on the computer won't hurt too much," he answered, seeing Mark just wanted to do something productive. "As long as it's not much…and stop if you get frustrated."

"I will. I am not actually doing any testing; I really can not right now. There are just a few things that need to be started in any application before we can begin any work. I am starting that part, so we do not miss any time once the hard tasks come."

"Well, I think you have been on the computer enough for today." Susan answered again while spooning more mashed steak and potatoes into his mouth.

Mark was silent, realizing his mother had taken the reins on the topic. He was quiet for the rest of the evening, rather than engaging in dinner conversation, he studied the family portrait on the wall, wishing to be back in the day when he could eat for himself; the day when his parents would let him decide his own schedule, when productive work was preferred over laying in front of the television.

Dinner was over and it was time for the evening ritual. This involved a trip to the restroom, changing clothes, and brushing Mark's teeth. He headed for the bathroom to get the routine over with. Susan followed him in, and they started with the teeth so foaming toothpaste would land on already soiled clothes. She brushed his teeth, which were generally clean from lack of use anyway, but disinfectant was still a grand idea. Since Mark could not spit, he would have to drool out the used toothpaste onto a rag in Susan's hand. The second humiliation in Mark's daily routine.

Next was the toilet. Mark was stripped from the waist down, lifted from the chair and placed in a cage-structure on the toilet that prevented him from falling off. She retreated to his room to fetch clothes returning in time to wipe and dress him.

"That's a lot of stuff on the computer screen, Mark," she said.

"Well, it is easy to type when I just need to think about it."

"But I don't want you working so much."

"It is not a lot! This is easy, like writing a shopping list! It is not work!" He yelled back in frustration.

"Still, no more time on the computer tonight. I turned it off."

"Mom, I was not done with that yet!" Mark yelled back.

"Well, you are for tonight!" She snapped as she slipped the shirt over his head getting ready to replace it with pajama tops. "It's family time now!"

So they left the bathroom and planted themselves in front of the television. It was not like the night before, a celebration of his regained ability to talk, but was oddly quiet, even more so than when Mark had to talk with the ACAT computer.

ЖĬ

After what seemed to be an eternity, the television program was over and Susan was ready for bed. Mark used the opportunity to visit his friend, Orion, on the back patio. He was desiring more time to brood by himself with the stars.

He reflected on the changes the last few days brought. Was the conflict increasing, or was he better able to voice it? Why was there such hostility to Mark working on a simple text file? For the first time in six months he felt like he had the opportunity to start regaining part of his functional life, but he was being held back from his attempts by the people who claimed to love him!

Still, the thought crossed Mark's mind that the conflict meant push back, and push back meant progress. The day prior to yesterday, Mark woke up with the bell and clumsily speaking with the ACAT:

"READY," contrasted with the "Time to get up," of today.

He had no conversation and merely wheeled himself to the table in the former day but the latter he asked what's for breakfast.

"TV" "BATHROOM" "HUNGRY" "FULL" were the belaboring words prior to the rich conversations possible today.

While he objected to his computer limits for now, he had more access through his device than he had for the last six months. Yes, the implant, the conflict, the speaker, the USB receiver. They were miracles with the hope of returning his life to something closer to normal. Mark had the computer to write ideas, the speaker to communicate them, and at least he did not need to learn how to program from scratch, but instead just needed to add a few tasks to his knowledge.

"Patient Zero," he said to himself through his speaker. "I am Patient Zero."

"Beep...beep...beep...," and the speaker was ready for bed.

"Hmm..." Mark again spoke to himself, "Maybe I should look to get a bigger battery for this thing."

He turned around pushing the patio door open, rolled in, and shut it again.

"I am beeping, Dad!" He announced as he rolled past the living room and into the bedroom.

The bedtime ritual was over fast, Mark was in bed, and the speaker and wheelchair began their nightly charge.

PART 2: BREAKTHROUGHS

7

Right at 9:00 AM, the sun began its rude wake up call, shining brightly into Mark's eyes. Unable to move enough to get out of its path, he called for his morning routine before the radio kicked on for the morning tunes. Susan was there in under a minute as if she had been preparing for the call just outside his room. The humiliating ritual was underway but Mark's focus on his daily project tasks made the humiliation more tolerable.

Breakfast concluded and Susan picked up the book laying on top of the dinning room cabinet.

"Let's get back to Mr. Asimov, Mark," she smiled, holding up a tattered library book.

"I was thinking, if you turn on my computer, I can read for myself today," he answered.

"I don't want you staring at the screen all day, Mark." she protested.

This illogical argument was a farce. The television had been on most of the day every single day for the last six months, and the present discussion was first time the merits or dangers of screen time arose since Mark was twelve years old.

"Mom, I sit in front of the television most of the day, and I have done so for the last several months. You have never had a problem with looking at screens since November. Why the concern now?"

Susan angrily tossed the book back on the cabinet, sensing his correct analysis, but trying to find a way to win the argument. "Go to your room!" She finally blasted like he was that twelve year old.

"Gladly!" He yelled back with just as much vigor.

Mark was reduced once again to being a twelve-year old boy. Screen times, yelling, and banished to the bedroom: a full recursion of past discipline. He watched his scrawny finger turn his wheelchair from the table and noticed that even in his body, he resembled that little twelve year old his mother was rebuking. Anger and frustration usurped the tears he wanted to flow from his eyes.

Mark closed the door with his wheelchair as hard as he could muster, but the slowness of his chair robbed him of the satisfaction of slamming it in his anger. He parked his chair at the desk by the lifeless computer and looked resentfully at the device he could finally use if only someone would turn it on for him. He felt he was being pulled into the arguments of yesterday, or rather, the fight was still lingering in the air. He finally had the ability to be productive, but he was being prevented from reading on his own, working on programs, or even playing a simple computer game.

The door suddenly opened and a red-faced Susan looked at Mark and the lifeless computer. Her red face was moist near the eyes, but she looked away. Without saying a word she walked over and powered on the computer. She watched the screen boot up and turned around leaving the room without a word. Mark issued a soft, "Thank you," but it was not heard over the loud thud of the slamming door.

Mark watched the door for a minute thinking that it might open again, but it did not. A small tear now rolled down his cheek. The desire to use the computer was overshadowed by conflict with his mother, but he finally turned to the computer and logged in. He first opened the documents and projects folder on the desktop to get back to the basic coding script he started. After staring at the screen for a few seconds, he thought back to their argument.

"It was not about working," he whispered to himself, just loud enough for him to hear the speaker, "it was about reading."

Mark closed the projects' folder, opened the applications window, and rolled over to Bookworm to read a book by himself for the first time since November. Since the argument was over Issac Asimov, he figured that would be a great place to start. Scrolling through the authors, he found his quarry and opened up *I, Robot* to get lost in the text for a while.

Ӝ

An hour had passed with *Robbie* on his mind when the door sprang open. "Did she ever knock anymore?" He thought to himself, but did not issue the command to the speaker.

"What are you working on, Mark?" His mom asked sheepishly, anticipating more conflict.

"I am reading. That is what I said I wanted to do. I just finished *Robbie*."

"*Robbie?*" She asked with more confidence this time.

"The first of the stories in *I, Robot*."

"Oh, that one with the little girl and the nanny robot. I remember now."

"It is sort of like an idea I have. And funny that Robbie can not talk because I did not have that in mind...with the speaker and all."

"What's your idea?" She was showing the first signs of being remotely supportive of his work.

Mark turned to the computer and pulled up the folder list, navigating to the projects folder and opening the document from yesterday titled ROBOT ASSISTANT.

"I think the first step I need to do is work to create a small test robot I can control with my mind. I can build him to help with simple tasks like picking up objects, opening doors; things that will just help regain the basic tasks. I think I will call him Robbie."

He went right under the objective line and created a character return typing with his mind, "His name is Robbie."

"That's a good name, Mark," Susan replied with a sigh half composed of joy but tainted by sorrow.

"I'll leave you to it," she walked out of the room, leaving the door open this time, giving him freedom to leave if he wanted to.

Mark admired the document for a bit longer before opening up the programming application he started earlier. The initial coding began with laying out the basic framework needed to program an arm, something he had done numerous times in the past with less critical applications. Now he just needed the device to start capturing the data to figure out how exactly to map his thoughts into a precision robotic arm.

His stomach reminded him of his hunger when he was finishing up the basic coding for the arm movement. His breakfast moved through his gut, and lunch was beckoning him.

Mark saved the documents, closed the files, and clumsily turned his chair to rejoin his mom in the living room. She was sitting on the couch, but was curiously not crocheting. She looked up to him with a somber glance.

"Mom, are you OK?" He said, breaking the dead silence in the room.

"Yes," she said, emboldening her demeanor.

"Can I get a smoothie for lunch?"

"Of course."

She stood up and walked just past him, touching his head on the way. Within a few seconds, he heard the sound of the cabinet opening and the blender coming down. Bananas were sliced, blueberries were dropped in and a small helping of milk was splashed over the fruit before the rest of the ingredients. The blender roared with the breaking and mixing of ice. The mixture was rolling and smooth, purple and rich. She poured it into Mark's red cup and inserted the straw before placing the cup into the cup holder on the chair. He rolled into position at the table to consume the drink.

"What is wrong, Mom? I can tell something is bothering you."

"Nothing, Mark."

"Mom. I am not twelve anymore." He thought back to his previous fight and his thoughts about being younger, how his earlier fight played out as if it were from the past. "Whatever it is, can we just talk about it? You have been quiet and teary all day…and not once did I see a crochet hook in your hand!"

"I don't know. Something's bothering me, but I just do not know exactly what it is."

"Well, this morning it was about reading. Are you bothered that I can read by myself now?"

"Maybe," there was a moments silence, then she continued, "I think it's neat that you can start doing more things. I like that, but I am also concerned about this implant. Do we know that it's safe?"

"Mom, that is what we are trying to figure out," he replied, "but I think you might be bothered that this implant is giving me back some of my independence." Now it was Mark's turn for a moment of silence as if they were dipping Hail Mary's to themselves between arguments.

"I still need you, Mom. I just need you in different ways. I know that since November you have taken on more of a nurse's role, but this implant might relieve me of the need for a nurse. Don't you want that for me?"

"Of course," she said, but unconvincingly, "I'm just concerned for the possible long term effects of this thing."

"Well, I understand that. But I want support in this research. And I really want to get to work soon!"

"Alright, Mark. I'll try to be more understanding of the research, but you need to understand that we don't want you to do anything strenuous until the doctors clear you for it."

"Well, can we at least talk to John to figure out exactly what I can and what I cannot do?"

"I think that can be arranged."

Ж

"Cuckoo, Cuckoo, Cuckoo, Cuckoo, Cuckoo." The clock was reminding Mark and Susan that Eric would be back from the hospital soon. Since clearing the air earlier, they were able to relax in each other's company in the living room again. Mark was productive in the early afternoon, working on some scripts, but he took some time with mom in front of the television as a break. Susan, meanwhile, was whipping out a blanket with the crochet hook occasionally looking up to see what the television program was about.

The garage door started growling as it slowly slid up its track. Mark, bored with the program on TV, rolled toward the kitchen to intercept his dad as he came in the side door.

"Hi Dad," he said once the door began its opening arc.

"Hi bud, how are you?"

"I am fine. How was work?"

"An emergency operation," he said sounding somewhere between bored and depressed. An emergency operation meant someone was hurt in an accident, and that always put Eric into a quieter mood than when he tended to scrapes and scratches.

"Is the person OK?" Mark asked, looking down at his own twisted body.

"Yes...we were able to stitch him up nicely and I think he will make a full recovery." Eric looked his son over, breathed out deeply and turned toward the hallway steps.

Mark knew immediately what he was thinking: "Why was I not OK?"

This put Mark to thinking some more about his first days back home from the hospital in November. While a few days prior he was looking forward to the luscious turkey dinner, but when he finally made it home, it was nothing but runny mashed potatoes. He loved talking to his family, but was suddenly robbed of that ability. He remembered back to that once-special holiday.

On the fated first holiday morning, he had to use the buzzer to ring for assistance. The talking speaker was brought to his bed where he would issue a few simple words.

"BATHROOM," and that was the start of the day. Where he used to talk about his favorite floats in the parade, this horrible day saw him sit in front of the television, almost lifeless except an occasional, "LIKE" or "COOL."

When the parade faded into the football game, even his sixteen-year-old self would still re-enact the touchdowns while dad would play the television announcer. But at seventeen, he sat helpless in a wheelchair, occasionally trying to smile, occasionally crying over his new helpless condition. The whole family was a wreck that day.

He missed walking up those steps at the end of the hall. Up the steps, along the banister, past his parents room, and into his own robotics cave. He had not been up those steps since then.

"Why was I not OK?" Mark thought to himself as a tear rolled down his cheek. He took one deep breath followed by another, trying to suppress his sadness. He could not hide his tears with his hands, so he decided instead to hide them with his absence. Mark opened up the patio door and rolled out to enjoy a bit of time outside where he drifted off to a nap in the cool of the early evening.

"Whoosh!"

Mark was startled awake by the patio door opening behind him.

"Time for dinner, honey," Susan said, going back to the boiling green beans but leaving the door open.

Mark rolled through the kitchen and took his place at the place-mat. He glanced back up at the family portrait and down to the fancy lace on his mat. Next, he glanced out the window to his left toward the woods until his dad entered the dining room with two glasses of water.

"Milk or water?" He asked for conversation only, knowing that water was always his answer. Mark never cared for plain milk as a beverage.

"Water, please," he said, smiling on the inside at the ability to communicate.

Susan came into the room with a plate of beans, ham, and potatoes which looked so enticing, as if beckoning him to try to eat. But that thought was laid to rest when a bowl of blended something was placed on his mat.

"What type of mush do I get today?" He asked, joking, but partially disgusted.

"You get the same thing we have! Ham, potatoes, and beans!"

"But, mom," he whined as jokingly as a child is serious, "I do not like it when my food touches!"

The dining room was instantly filled with well-needed laughter, lifting all moods in its wake. They all looked at each other, breathed out the last of the bad mojo and proceeded on with dinner.

"Dad, can we talk to John about what I can do on the computer and what I cannot before the two-week evaluation?"

Eric looked first to Susan to wait for her objection, but she just spooned some mush into Mark's mouth as if he did not say anything. Finally, he wanted to be sure to not be on his wife's bad side, he directed to her, "What do you think, Susan?"

She pulled the mostly empty spoon from Mark's mouth and placed it back into the bowl and picked up her own fork to attack the ham. "I think it is a good idea to find out what he can and can't do before the checkup."

Eric was surprised by her sudden support of Mark's efforts. After the temporary confusion faded, he agreed a call would be a good idea so everyone was on the same page as to the extent of work that Mark could do before he was cleared to go back to the lab.

8

"What are the results of the latest tests?"

"Well, the signals are being received by the subject, but they're leaving behind traces in the system logs. We're trying to prevent that all together, sir." The young coder swallowed hard. He was stuck working late again in the programmer's office, which seemed darker after hours when everyone else had gone home.

"I'd say to remove logs altogether, but without'em we will be open to immediate scrutiny. Can we disable logs based on the specific hardware?" The older, pudgy man inquired as he loosened his already loose tie more before sliding it over his neck, as if unleashing himself from his other duties.

"That's what we are trying now, sir. I am inserting some code to search for the hardware logging the event. We need to find and block 'SIDTB' from logging. But if anyone audits the code, they will be able to see the exclusion. It will be pretty obvious certain hardware inputs are being ignored by the log."

"We will just need to compile the driver and not have the specific code on the server. I want the code myself, with and without the device logging, but put it on a USB drive for me, and not on the company server. I'll tell you when to put it up there...When will you be done with the code?"

"Hopefully within the hour. I can't be late for dinner again or I'll hear it from the old lady!"

"Well, finish up in that time or you'll hear it from me, too. I need to go make some calls." The man finished massaging his mustache and grabbed his overcoat from the chair, and abruptly left the room, closing the door loudly behind him inducing a flinch in the coder. The young man breathed out a sigh before turning back to the computer screen.

"Few more lines, and I'm outta here," he said to his empty bottle of orange soda laying sideways on the desk.

He pecked away at the keyboard some more, finally letting out a deep breath while leaning back in his chair. The C++ compiler processed the code and spit out the final drivers. The drivers were loaded into the test system and the update was run on the computer connected to the display monitor looking over a rat cage.

"Let's see if you work now," he said to himself as the computer rebooted. The test script worked as he planned, so he copied the code from the computer onto a USB drive on the desk and deleted the copy from the computer.

"Sir!" He yelled out, heading into the manager's office.

"Is it done?"

"Yes. I ran the test protocol. The rat still seemed to behave a little off, but there are no logs from the hardware now, only the signal input as requested."

"And the drive?"

The young coder extended his hand, a drive was wedged between his thumb and index finger, "Right here."

"And this is the only copy?" He asked while snatching the prize from the young man's hand.

"Yes, sir, I deleted the working file from the computer."

"Excellent, I guess you don't get any rebukes from me or your wife. You can go now."

Ж

Modernized classical music rang lightly through the speakers where David approached the doors to Giordano's, the fanciest Italian restaurant in town. The dimly lit waiting room was attended by a tux-clad maitre d who promptly opened the door for him while announcing, "Welcome to Giordano's, sir. Has the rest of your party arrived?"

"I am meeting a Mr. Davis, has he arrived?"

"Very good sir, right this way. Mr. Davis arrived moments ago."

The maitre d led the way to a corner booth where two wine glasses had already been filled with a deep red wine.

"Thank you, sir," David said taking the seat opposite his old college roommate.

"Tyler. How are you, my friend?"

Tyler lowered the menu, exposing his green eyes and cracking a smile through his freckly face. He ran his hands through his short red hair and yawned.

"Too busy like usual, but still living the dream! How're you this fine Friday evening?"

"Well, new course material is over, now it's onto finals and grading. Once that's done, the summer of our most intense research project shall begin!"

"You're still blocking out 1999, aren't you?"

They both chuckled. Not only were they roommates in college, but they also took nearly the same block of courses, being perpetual study and lab partners. The inside joke, of course, referred to that insane coding project for their capstone research, which started in the last summer before graduation.

"Well, no sleep…no girls…nothing but computers and junkyard parts…yep, still blocking that out!"

They had a chuckle, both reaching for their wine glass at the same time and lightly taping them together, causing a light ring to emanate from the center of their table.

"For Mark," David said as they each sipped from the excessively dry wine in their glasses.

"And how is our Patient Zero?"

"It was truly the most amazing thing I ever saw, Tyler. I called Wednesday night expecting to talk to Eric and Susan about how the operation went. Mark was on speaker phone and talking for the first time. It was quite incredible." David looked directly into Tyler's eyes, capturing all the attention he could while explaining the medical breakthrough that evening.

"I knew he'd pick up the ability to talk naturally. That is exactly the type of result we expected from the diagnostic data we collected from the rats. Anything he could do with his motor cortex will come just as naturally. We have to be careful, though, not to cross the signals, so we do not make him kick when he should be raising his hand!" Tyler said, confident of the hardware.

"Yes, he picked up using the HID just as quickly. I dropped it off yesterday and installed the drivers. He was instantly able to login and use the computer and mouse inputs just by thinking about it."

"When will he be able to start the research?" Tyler was anxious to get started on capturing signals from a creature whom could communicate what signals were trying to be sent!

"The doctors want about two weeks before they will clear him for lab research. In the meantime, I think he can do some light computer work, so he's going to start working on that."

"Excellent. And how is the speaker working out?" Tyler responded

David answered, "Just fine. He can talk just like a normal person."

"What else has he been able to do with it?"

David's eyes took on a puzzled look, so Tyler continued, "What do you mean?"

"That thing's a full fledged smart speaker. He can use the wake word 'Synaptergate' to ask it anything, get simple facts, create lists to dump to the computer. It's not just a device for talking, it's a full access computer itself, well, once it is on a network anyway."

"I don't think Mark knows any of that. I'll let him know when I talk to him next. Speaking of which, do we have an update on the hardware to collect the signals?"

"We have a few bugs in the system. It looks like some software bug is sending some signals back into the rats causing them to behave a little out of the ordinary, but it does appear to be rare. Our coders in the back lab have isolated the software bug and are reportedly fixing it now. We're working on another test, presently. The results will be in by Wednesday."

"That's fine. I cannot devote the time to it until these cursed finals are over anyway, and Mark can't get to work until sometime after that on doctor's orders. But I'll give him the update and tell'em about the speaker functions. Do we have documentation on that?"

"It's all on the central server, so you can access it there," then he added, "you better give him the heads up about the extra signals, so he can tell us if anything like that happens."

The waiter arrived at the table, but waited for a conversation break, "Are you gentlemen ready to order?"

"Yes," Tyler said addressing him directly. The server took their orders and stiffly strode back to the kitchen.

"Tell me more about these signals, Tyler. What are they from, what're they doing?"

"Well, I'm not sure where they are from. I looked at the logs and see a hardware device that is sending signals into the implant, but I am not sure what those signals could be doing. In the video tests, the rats look to be confused. They eat but when you think they should drink, they stare between the food and water bottle like they are forgetting what they want to do. They just look…I don't know…confused?"

"Do you think it's signals being sent, or biofeedback of some sort?"

"I would say biofeedback except the log shows input from a transmitter of some sort. I was not able to isolate what it was exactly."

"Is there a MAC address?"

"No, just a code. SIDTB is the only thing showing up as a hardware component."

David rubbed his chin in deep thought, "How are they looking to deal with it?"

"Not sure. They said it could be a bug in the software, so they are working late tonight to isolate the bug. I'll let you know what I find out as soon as I have the info."

9

On Saturday morning, Mark awoke in the usual way to music and then calling for the morning routine after his binge of classic rock was complete. While his parents were busy with household chores, he was hammering away at some document layouts and planning more experiments. He was slaving over PDFs of Raspberry Pi boards, looking at some course notes on the computer, and shuffling documents around into file folders. Mark was truly happy for the first time in a while as if his various disabilities were fading away.

"Ding dong din don...Ding Dong DIN DON." The visitor at the door was unexpected.

"I got it!" Eric yelled out from his spot at his desk. He opened the door just feet from his wooden chair.

"Professor, come on in. And I forget your name." He said to a second visitor.

"Micheal," he said in a familiar voice just within range of Mark's hearing.

Micheal was the only student who visited Mark last November. He made the occasional trip over, but the visits faded as communication and ability had ceased. Micheal was not a total stranger to the house; he and Mark would often play some Black Ops together on breaks from their schoolwork. Now, however, Mark could at least talk to his friend.

When he heard Micheal's friendly voice, Mark saved his documents. He instinctively backed up his wheelchair just enough to clear the desk. The motor in his chair whirred as he spun around, heading for the living room.

"Micheal!" He yelled from the speaker.

"Wow...that new voice transplant...much better than that old squeaky thing you used to have!" He joked, getting right back into the old days of casual insults between friends.

"Ha, ha, ha!" Mark said. He smiled and moved the wheelchair close to Micheal's hand for clumsy one-way fist bump. "You have got to see how fast I can use the computer! I will be the one typing the results now. You will be too slow with that cumbersome two handed typing you do!"

Micheal followed Mark into his room to see the computer and see for himself how the implant HID functioned.

"Sorry for the unannounced visit," the professor started, still in the living room with Eric.

"No problem at all. Thanks for bringing Micheal by. Mark seems to be happy to see him today since they can finally use the computer and talk again."

"I stopped by to update Mark on some information. I talked to Tyler last night. It turns out the speaker can be connected to the Internet to do basic searches. I didn't know about it when we sent the speaker to the hospital to sync it to the implant, but I have the documents for it. I didn't think Mark had email on his computer yet, but I wanted him to know what else the speaker can do."

"Well, he'll be glad to know about it. You can give it to him today. Will it be complicated to set up? You know how we are with computers. Once Mark, well, you know," he stopped with a somber tone before tripping over words, "we have been lost ever since," he finally completed.

"I can get everything hooked up if you want. I'll just need the WiFi passwords."

"Oh, they are over here," Eric said turning to the desk. He opened up the bottom cabinet drawer and shuffled through some folders. "Ah, here they are."

Eric stopped in his tracks looking down to the scribbling of random digits, all placed there by his now motor-deficient son. He was momentarily lost in his thoughts, forgetting he was in the company of friends. He snapped back to his senses and raised his countenance back up before handing the folder to David.

"We talked things over here last night, and we'll be heading to the hospital lab this afternoon to talk to John, the head surgeon, who'll let us know exactly what Mark can and cannot do. Depending on what he says, we may be able to let Mark do some early research and work, but probably just from home. If the doctor clears it, we'll have him online soon."

"That's great!" David said, "We just need the basics done now. Tyler is still working on a bug in the software that collects the signals and it's expected in a week or so, and I am in finals period, so lots of reviews, student visits and grades, so we will not be ready for a couple weeks in the lab."

"I think he's been doing some document layouts. I don't understand it, but it looks like just writing words on files, so we said he can keep doing that unless John tells him to stop."

After a pause, Eric continued, "Do you two want to stay for lunch? We have plenty and Mark would be glad to have friends over."

"I think we can do that. Micheal and I were going to grab lunch anyway before heading back to the college. As long as he is good with staying, we'll stay."

The two walked to Mark's room where he was showing off his newfound computer skills to Micheal, who was gawking over the newfound input speeds.

"Micheal, we can stay for lunch if you want," said the professor, both announcing his presence in the room, and asking about plans for lunch.

"Can I get one of these implants, too?" He replied as if he had not heard the question about lunch.

"Only if you get traumatic brain injuries." Mark replied.

"Have a hammer?" Micheal retorted.

Eric just shook his head and left the room. "No self-inflicted brain injuries in the house," he casually barked as if it were an actual rule.

"Lunch, Micheal? Do you want to stay?"

"Sure."

"OK, on to business. Mark, your speaker can do more than just let you talk. I found out from Tyler yesterday that it's actually a smart speaker. It can be connected to the Internet and queried for information. We only have a search function built into it right now, but you can ask it information and get back answers from online. They are working on an update to process emails, take notes, and more. Want to see what it does?"

"Sure," said Mark.

David opened the folder on the desk, "We need to start with the wireless."

Mark recognized his old handwriting in an instant and ordered the page to be flipped over, as he knew just where the passwords were.

"Actually, we first need to know how to program this thing."

He took a red USB flash drive from his pocket and handed it to Micheal who was directly in front of the tower. The drive was inserted into the front port of the computer and the blue light started flashing.

"Copy that document to your docs, Mark. It's the instruction manual for the speaker."

He issued several computer commands with his mind and the file manager instantly appeared and a PDF was copied to his documents folder under 'implant'. The PDF was merely the careless output of a raw text document.

"Based on the documentation, this thing is not ready for the public market yet." Mark joked, looking at the computer programmer's seemingly random notes and commands spewed forth, all being totally accurate but completely useless to the muggle computer masses. But these men were not the masses. They quickly found the commands to put the device on the network.

"Press and hold the button for three seconds. The device will beep."

"Say the encryption type. Wait for the beep."

"Say the password. Say 'cap' before a capital letter, just say the letter for lowercase."

About ten minutes later of clumsily trying to say commands and giggling out the wrong codes, the unruly beast was finally on the network.

"Definitely not ready for the public market yet...does Synaptergy want that feedback, too?" Micheal laughed in relief that the device was finally connected.

The document was consulted again to find the instructions on how to use the smart component. The device was only set to use with the implant, so a random person in the room could not access the network. But Mark, being the device match owner, could think "Synaptergate," and then issue a command with his mind.

"Well, let's ask it something," Micheal finally said.

"Synaptergate...Something."

"Something what?" the speaker replied.

"Hmmm...Let's try this. Synaptergate...search Something."

"Something is a song performed by the Beatles. It was written by George Harrison and released on the 1969 album titled Abbey Road."

"It certainly knows what Google is," David sighed in relief that it was doing something.

"Synaptergate...what is the current temperature."

"The current temperature is 16 degrees Celsius or 61 degrees Fahrenheit."

"Synaptergate…what is the weather forecast?"

"Today is mostly sunny with a 10% chance of rain into the evening hours with a low near 6 degrees Celsius or 43 degrees Fahrenheit. Tomorrow will be warmer with a high near 18 degrees Celsius or 65 degrees Fahrenheit. It will be sunny."

"This is handy. I will never be without useless facts or weather forecasts again!"

At the conclusion of these tests, it was time for lunch and then off to visit John at the hospital.

10

Eric drove by muscle memory to his reserved parking space at the hospital. Mark glanced from tree to tree while the van rolled toward the parking spots. The red buds on the branches reminding Mark of his own personal unfolding since the operation.

Eric eased the van into the parking spot, and Mark's view was obstructed by John's truck, which pulled in right next to them about the same time.

"Thanks for making time today, John," said Mark, while they were all getting out of their cars.

"No problem. I'm a little curious how things look myself. Just don't tell the guys at Synaptergy. They'll not like off-schedule checkups!"

"If it means I get a few more days of work, I will keep my mouth shut!"

John broke a smile at Mark, happy to see him in such good spirits after months of difficult testing. "Well, shall we head in?"

"Let us do this," Mark said, charging forward in his wheelchair.

"Well, I think he's anxious," Susan said, grabbing Eric's hand and walking behind the doctor.

The white, sanitized examination room Mark had visited hundreds of times before somehow seemed brighter today. Maybe it was the excitement about things he could do with the help of the implant, or the progress of his recovery so far.

John first started with an examination of the surgical region, still readily visible after only a few days of hair growth. Eric also took a turn examining the surgical region, but neither doctor was able to tell an operation had even taken place.

"OK, Mark, basic reflex tests that we both know will do nothing."

John tested the reflexes as he did before, with Mark able to at least communicate feeling now, but still, as predicted, no result.

"Let's get wired up for the EEG."

Mark hated the paste needed to get the electrodes to stick to his head and provide signal transfer because he was not able to scratch after the electroencephalogram was complete. But the joy of his progress overcame the hate of the uncomfortable paste. He was wired up for the test, which was underway before he realized it. These results also looked normal.

"Well, Mark, I'm not seeing anything out of the ordinary here, but we still can't let you do a full load of work. This is mostly because Synaptergy insists on the full two-week waiting period before we do any official tests for clearance. These are your limits: You can work on the computer for up to four hours a day, but I don't want you to have the stimulation of the Internet yet. This means documents preps and anything else you can do without the Internet. Also, don't do experiments with what the implant can do, just keep things basic. Any issues, headaches, or anything else unusual, your dad needs to know immediately. Any questions?"

"Does that four hour limit include reading and video games?"

"Let's say no, but limit your games to about an hour a day for now, and reading non-work-related also to an hour. Anything else?"

"Why can't I get the Internet yet?"

"There are a few reasons. First, it can actually rewire your brain, and we don't want that to happen until we know the implant is done seating itself. Second, we do not want it to slip that we looked at you at all yet. Third, I do not want the temptations to do any collaborations at this time. Got it?"

"Yes, sir."

"What about the speaker, John?" Eric asked.

"What about it?"

Eric explained the Internet connected possibilities and how David gave him the information about how to put the speaker online. Mark chimed in with search queries about weather and miscellaneous search terms.

John casually massaged his chin while listening to their description of the speaker, trying to make up his mind. "Let's disconnect it for now. I want to err on the side of caution." Directing now at Mark, "Is that OK with you?"

"There goes my new job of weather forecaster," Mark joked, still in good spirits, "but as long as I can use the rest of the computer I will give that up."

Eric looked at his watch and then glanced over to Susan, "Alright then, if we are done, we need to get home and get ready for tonight. Thanks again for taking the time, and we'll see you this evening."

"See you then, Eric," he replied, wiping down the examination room.

They left the hospital hastily, to get ready for the evening's plans. Mark was comfortable with his limits, but hoped his dad might argue his case more than he did.

Ж

The family piled back into the van again, heading to Kristy's house this time. They rolled up to Kristy's driveway and stopped close to the steps. Eric pressed the foot petal for the e-brake, the harsh clicking noise signaling Susan to open the sliding door. She started undoing buckles, holding Mark's wheelchair in place, and freeing him to roll down the ramp arriving at the bottom of the insurmountable steps. He had nothing left to do but wait for the humiliating task of being lifted out of the chair and up the steps. Sam and Eric muscled the heavy weight of the electric wheelchair up into the house. After the ordeal, Mark was returned to his seat now inside the living room.

"Well, I think you have everything, Mark." Eric offered in place of saying goodbye, glancing to his watch in anticipation of leaving.

"I love you, Honey," Susan said, kissing his cheek, but hastily standing back up, heading to the door he thought, but Grandma-instinct took over, and she walked to Emily, picking her out of the swing. She looked over the baby and started speaking in 'baby tongue,' goo-gooing and gah-gahing. The baby responded in kind and added giggles to the mix like the two were having a conversation unknown to the rest of the room.

"Honey, we need to get going," Eric said, admiring his watch again from the front door.

"I'll take her, Mom," Kristy said retrieving the baby and restoring her to the swing.

"Bye everyone," Susan said, heading out the door behind Eric. Within a minute, the minivan was pulling out toward the sunset.

"How's your week been, Mark?" Kristy asked.

"Good. I found out the speaker can connect to the Internet and make me a meteorologist...but the doctor does not want me to use it yet. Also, I have a device that can be used to control the computer which is so much faster than I have ever been able to use it in the past!"

"How difficult is it to use?" Sam was listening, but finally joined into the conversation.

"Not hard at all. I just need to think about what I want to do. Well, not really think it, but play it out in my mind. You will need to come and check it out."

The conversation faded into documents and programs, things that went above Kristy's head, so she went to the kitchen to start the meal. Sam was somewhat familiar with the approach Mark was trying to take in creating his robotics, but he focused more on the hardware implementation. He never did the research type of work Mark was studying in designing how the systems worked, but he knew how to take the schematics and build the hardware with perfect precision.

"Sam, you can build robots, right?" Mark had the flash of an idea hit his mind. What if Sam could help in this project.

"Well, that's what I do day in and out, so, yeah."

"I am working on building a robot I will call Robbie who is going to be controllable with my mind. I want him to be an assistant to do basic tasks for me. If I come up with the plans, can you build it?"

"Robbie?" He asked, "Is that short for something?"

"No. Robbie from *I, Robot*."

"The robot's name was Sonny, I think," Sam argued back.

Mark tried to shake his head in subtle disapproval, "Sonny was the robot in the MOVIE, Robbie was in the BOOK," he corrected and then paused, "Can you help with it?"

"Yes, I can most likely help with creating it if I can get some schematics. Doesn't your lab do that, though?"

"Sort of. We have the parts, and we can do crude modeling, but we cannot build them for production quality or weather resistance. We have a team at Synaptergy that we are supposed to give the plans to, but I want to keep a copy of them and work on regular improvements personally."

"Well, I can certainly help with that part. If you have the code working to make the basics function, I will be able to see the flaws and provide input on the design."

They discussed the plans and requirements for the commercial robots late into the evening. Mark was thinking more than ever about how his implant could help him to regain his life, and with Sam, he could actually produce equipment that could be used in the real world.

"If you gentlemen are done talking shop, I have dinner about ready." The men were so engrossed in robotics conversation that they did not hear the blender run or any of the other sounds Kristy made while creating a small feast.

"I guess we will talk more about it later. Let's just have some dinner and watch a movie for the rest of the evening."

11

The next several days included the normal monotony of daily routines combined with the excitement of document preparations. The thoughts trapped in Mark's mind finally had a means of escape, and many ideas were written down, waiting to be analyzed by the lab team when the bulk of the project finally began. Tomorrow was the final appointment to determine if the doctors would clear Mark to return to the lab for more research. Like a kid waiting for that cursed Christmas Eve to give way to the glorious morning, today could not pass fast enough for Mark.

He was once again visiting Orion on the back porch reflecting on the last few weeks. He experienced the anticipation of the surgery, talking with the aid of the new speaker, using the computer better than he ever had in the past, and turning his mind once again to his research.

Mark even thought back to his relationship with his parents, how his mother had now embraced his return to research. But he still felt a strain with his dad. They had a few more conversations, but they always seemed too surface, like their rich past relationship lay somewhere just beyond a dense fog. He tried with his might to piece together the last talk they ever had with his real voice.

"What do you think robots can't replace in the hospital, Dad?" He concluded his question with a gulp of hot chocolate from his favorite green mug.

"There's a lot a robot can't do. I'm not sure they could figure out triage. Also, robots can't have the compassion it takes to visit people who are sick in bed, or to deliver bad news to family members. Sure they can see needs and provide the best health care, but there's a lot more to a healthy person than patching up wounds. We need the compassion that only comes from the heart to see emotional needs." Eric paused at the end of his discussion to now sip his cup in turn.

"Don't you think it is possible to train a robot to do those things?"

"I doubt it," said Eric, "compassion isn't a matter of knowledge. It's a matter of heart. A robot can have all the knowledge in the world, but they can't ever be given a genuine heart that understands emotional pain. Take

Robbie, in *I, Robot.* He doesn't latch onto Gloria because of love or devotion in the way we stick tight as a family. He latches onto her because that is what he's programmed to do. There is a difference between a program directing actions through a machine that automatically obeys those commands, whatever they are, and a heart that can choose to stop caring but refuses to do so. That is compassion."

"I guess I agree. There are some limitations. I wonder how we could get a robot to have compassion, though," said Mark.

"I'm not sure it is worth it. What's the point of real relationships if we all just started turning our devotion to robots?"

"I guess we would probably stop having relationships with people because we would never have conflict with a robot." Mark paused at that, reflecting in his own mind. He figured the loss of human relationships would probably be bad, but what would be wrong with a relationship without conflict?

Eric, seemingly able to read his son's mind, answered those objections. "That's the problem, Mark. Without conflict, we never grow, we never change our mind, we never have anything to look back on to point to progress. No one likes the fight in the middle of it, but we want to see how our love grows deeper as we find our way out of conflict together. That's something we cannot do with a robot. I will die happy if we never pretend we gave consciousness to a machine."

As if his statement was the conclusion of the matter, Eric pushed back the rest of the hot chocolate. Mark followed suit. They both knew this was the perfect place to end their talk, but neither knew it would be the last they would share while Mark had control over his now wrecked body.

Glancing up again to Orion, and satisfied by the memory of their last talk, he thought back to the lessons to be learned. His father did still love him, or he would have left. But he also remembered the part about conflict. They were still in it, but Mark wanted out. He said goodnight to his heavenly friend and turned the chair around making his way into the house. He approached the desk in the living room, knowing his dad would be there in the way a predictable drunk has a regular bar stool. Eric was there, studying the budget.

"Do you remember our last talk in November?"

"Yes, Mark."

"I was thinking about it today. We were talking about conflict, and struggles, and growing, and how a robot can not learn those things."

"I remember," and again, he fell silent, not even looking up.

"Dad, I feel like we are in conflict now, and I want to move past it. I can not keep up this research without help and ideas. I miss our talks and I want to know why you seem distant. I know you still love me; you are still here. But why have you stopped talking?"

"I still wish I could have done more." He answered with a deep breath across the top of a water bottle he was clutching as if it were a child's favorite toy.

After a minute, Mark broke the silence, "What do you mean, 'if you could do more?'"

Eric, still somber began tearing up. He whispered, "I was there when you were brought in. I was waiting for the ambulance in my normal place waiting for a 'juvenile in critical condition' as was reported by the medic on the radio. The door was opened but Mike was the first one in. He told me to run into the O.R. to wait for him to bring in the patient, so I did. I went in and started prepping as he usually does for me. John came in and took me to the staff break room. I thought I saw you in the corner of my eye, but I must have been mistaken. John confirmed to my horror that it was you. He would not let me see you, but I wanted to. If I was there, maybe I could have done more."

Eric laid his head into his hands, elbows resting on a stack of bills. He sobbed in his grief until a single tear dripped onto the bill and absorbed into the paper.

"And you feel guilty? Is that why you have seemed distant for the last few months?"

"Yes," he whispered.

"Dad, there was nothing you could do. All the scans *you* confirmed showed all the damage was done *before* I arrived at the hospital! There is nothing you could have done. There is nothing anyone could have done to make my body work. We cannot go back, we have to move forward! We have hope for the first time." He paused for a moment. "Dad, I do not blame you, and I want my dad back. I want back the man I look up to, and the one who listens to my ideas and who makes me hot chocolate."

Eric was silent in thought, and the ticking clock counted the ten long seconds. He finally said, "I know. I've so many times consoled parents and said there's nothing they could have done, but until it happens, I guess no one believes it." He sniffled some more before continuing, "I guess I finally understand a little better how a mom and dad feel when I have to give them very bad news about their child."

"Well, Dad, with your help, maybe we can bring hope to the world through this technology. Can we start talking about it some more?" Mark encouraged.

"Yes, as long as we can talk about the rest of life, too."

"It is a deal." Mark confirmed as he sat motionless watching for his father's next move.

Eric gulped down the rest of his water as if it were a shot of whiskey at the conclusion of a hard decision, "Whelp, I think it is time for bed."

"I love you, Dad!" Mark inserted, wanting to be the one to end this conversation. Dad knew the intention and just smiled.

12

"You're Out!" It was hard to tell which random voice in the crowded gym yelled at Mark. The school was one of the few places dodge ball had not yet been restricted for making kids feel bad. Mark knew he was out even before he heard the cries so he automatically proceeded to the sit-out line next to the other athletically challenged kids in physical education. He did not care that his performance was poor; he knew he could overpower his peers in any academic challenge, and most of them knew it, creating a stalemate of respect among his peers. Mark was not snobbish about his college courses, but neither did he hide his ability when the time came for answers in his high school courses.

He intentionally scheduled phys ed as early in the day as possible to get it over with, providing more focus on difficult courses later. Not to mention he also only attended half a day in his senior year so that he could take robotics and some gen ed requirements for his associates degree at the university. He liked his schedule, which was more like college and less like high school.

"Hit the showers!" The coach called out five minutes before the bell. Not that anyone in the school ever actually took showers after gym class, but the coach was so used to that expression for his sports teams that it became his iconic way of ending the class period.

Mark shuffled into the locker room with the rest of the kids and changed into his beige sweater and jeans to get on with the rest of his morning classes, next of which was history. He hated history, putting up with it just enough to collect his passing grade to fulfill the requirements. If it were up to Mark, he would not even take such a class, but he figured the high school version would be easier than the college version, and either one gave him the check mark for his subject requirement. He watched the clock tick away, and after a disengaging lecture on the history of the industrial revolution, he walked out of class for what he did not know was his very last time. It was time to head to the college, but first he needed to stop by his locker to drop off the things he did not need outside these walls.

As usual, the locker put up a fight, but he struggled his way in.

"What's up, Mark?" A familiar voice called out to him.

"Oh, hi Tim. Not much, just getting ready to head to the college."

Tim was Mark's oldest friend. They lived pretty close by, on the same bus route, and were certainly within biking distance. They spent their elementary years goofing off, and then the middle school years getting into the usual boy trouble that seems to be required to enter adolescence. Now in high school, they still talked occasionally but did not have any classes together. Since Mark left school before lunch, they only caught each other in the halls and the occasional time playing video games over the weekends.

"Want to get together this weekend for some Borderlands?" Asked Tim.

Mark smiled enthusiastically, "Yeah, sounds good! Just come over when you can. I should be around all weekend."

"Alright, see you then! I gotta run…chemistry's across the school from here!"

"LATER!" Mark yelled while Tim was assimilated into the sea of students like water being absorbed into a rushing river.

Mark finally slammed the locker door closed when the bell rang the warning sound for the students to be on their way to class. He looked down to his phone to check the time. Had he spent that much extra time fighting the locker today? He rushed toward the front door to where the bus picked up a few other students heading to town on early release. He pushed through the door, bruising his arm in his rush, but the bus was already turning down onto the main road to the college.

Ӝ

"We're here, Mark!" Eric announced loudly jarring Mark from his daydream.

"What 'cha thinking about, Mark?" Susan said noticing he seemed a little dazed.

"Nothing," he paused to orient his thoughts, "Just hoping we can get back to work."

"Well, that's what we will know in a bit," said Eric.

Eric parked the car in his regular doctor's parking spot out of instinct, and they began their task of getting Mark out of the van and into John's office. Mark was admiring the young, spouting leaves that had replaced the red buds that were on the branches last time he was here.

The tests were as boring as usual; the same look here look there, and testing reflexes. The final test would be the CT scan to see if there was any brain injury from the implant or operation.

"Well, Mark," John started, "the scans will take a few days to come back, but I don't see any reason why you can't have some freedom. You need to promise that no matter where you are or who you are with, anything that seems to not feel right you need to stop and call me or your dad. As long as you do that, unless the scan shows me something concerning, you can do any amount of work you want."

Mark lingered in silence for a few seconds, processing his emotions. He was unable to smile, or jump, or express emotion beyond what the speaker was now able to convey, so it was a sudden rejoicing of words with a cornucopia of expression of thanks and acknowledgments.

"That's great, John!" Eric followed, "Let's celebrate!"

"Chocolate milkshakes?" Mark asked.

"Absolutely!" And the family was off to grab some milkshakes and head to the local computer store to find an Ethernet cable long enough to connect Mark's computer to the Internet.

Ӂ

"Can we stop by the college?" Mark asked while they were piling into the van with the Ethernet cable resting in Mark's lap. "I want to stop by David's office and tell him the good news in person."

"I don't mind, do you honey?" Eric confirmed with his wife.

She answered, "Let's do it. It is Mark's day!" So they drove over to the university, making the twisting turns through campus for first time since November.

Thanks to the handicap parking sticker, they were able to park in the spot right next to the door of the lab building. Mark guided them to the door of the building with the ramp and through to the heart of the lobby where the elevator was situated. They piled into the elevator and headed to the second floor. When the doors slide open, the institutional scent caught their nose and they were glancing on David's dark office.

"Where's David?" Susan said with concern in her voice as she looked at the dark office.

"He is in class, Mom. He should be back in about ten minutes. But Micheal will probably be in the lab."

His wheelchair motor roared up as he rolled down the right corridor out of the elevator heading toward the lab, but was stopped by a familiar voice calling out, "Hey loser. What're you doing here?!"

Mark's chair spun around swiftly causing Eric to jump out of the way, "Micheal! How is it going!"

"Good. Just getting back from a late lunch. Did you want to come by and visit the old stomping grounds?"

"Well, that, and some news. I can come back to work any time."

"Follow me, then."

Mark followed his friend into the lab. They passed each row, each of which was ignored by Mark, except the third row that led to his old desk, which was now occupied by a stranger with his nose in a laptop. The young student was so used to people walking by that he never looked up. Just beyond the divider wall where Brett used to have an office space was a newly renovated desk built slightly higher for wheelchair access. The window looked out over the courtyard and a new computer was sitting lifelessly.

"Let me do the honors," Micheal said, pushing the power button on the front of the tower. The surge of energy caused a sudden growl of the various fans and boot up noises, then the login screen appeared and Micheal typed the password.

"There you go. She's yours to fly!"

Mark's instincts kicked in and he opened the user settings to set his own password. Within another few seconds a terminal window was booted and a host of packages were being installed getting ready for Mark to start working.

The computer command interface began its work, so Mark spun around to look at the new setup. His lab bench was already full of partially completed projects as if he had already been working. The window provided a great view out into the quad, and the desk behind was overflowing with document printouts and other robotics paraphernalia.

"Who is in the desk behind me?"

"Oh, that's me. I took up your bench space with some projects, so we could store some extra stuff for the project on my bench. It's all robotics parts from Synaptergy. They haven't spared any expense with this research."

"Well, that is good. I really only need the computer right now anyway. I do not intend on needing the bench space any time soon. But if I do, I will just run you over and take it!"

"Fair enough," he countered, then changing the subject, "Wait here. David should be back by now."

Micheal left the lab and headed out to the office, intercepting David who was just returning from class.

"There's something urgent in the lab that needs your attention, professor," he called out while the key was just twisting open the lock.

"OK. Let me put this down and I'll be right there," he said with a sigh. He then silently continued to himself, "I only wanted a few minutes of down time!"

He discarded his briefcase onto the office chair and started up the computer for the day, but left it on the login screen, composed himself with an intentional positive attitude, and strode into the lab. David walked into Mark's half of the lab only to see Mark, Susan, and Eric admiring the view.

"Look at you!" David called out.

"Hi David. The desk is perfect. And we are ready to get back to work!"

13

Mark started official lab work the following day. The schedule they all agreed on was a month of working at home in the mornings with travel to the lab for a few hours just after lunch. On the first morning, Mark connected to the university VPN to transfer the documents he already completed to the lab servers, and then he pulled several files he needed to read down to his computer. He reasoned the most prudent use of time would be reading the Man Pages for the hardware that was to be used to collect signals from the implant. He studied the documents and took simple notes as a quick reference guide. After an hour of flipping through the procedures, he uploaded his help file to the server and stopped for lunch.

His blended mash was less than appetizing, but his desire to work in the lab overcame his unvoiced objections. Promptly after he was done, Susan drove him to the university. She saw him up to the lab door and kissed him goodbye much to his dismay.

"Mooommm," the speaker whined.

"OK," she said in reply, "I will be by about 4:30 to pick you up."

Mark headed into the lab and made his way to the bench where his computer was waiting for a login. He retrieved the necessary files and reviewed the protocols again, finally announcing to Micheal, who was shuffling papers behind him, that he was ready to give it a go.

"Alright. Head down to the computer at the last row and wait for David. He wants to be there for the first equipment run," Micheal instructed.

Mark headed to the computer with the hardware interface while Micheal fetched David to get started on the most anticipated experiment Mark had ever performed.

"Are we ready?" David said grabbing the seat at the computer while opening up the terminal to start the application.

"Ready here," Micheal echoed, watching an oscilloscope screen that resembled the EKG of a dead man.

"OK here," Mark confirmed on his end.

"Test 1: random attempts to move limbs," David recorded.

Mark started the actions of his dreams: he attempted to stand, reach out his hand, kick the air, wiggle his toes. He hated that nothing happened to his limbs but was excited to see the mass of peaks from the formerly flat-lined scope. It was all over the chart. The positive control for collecting signals from the implant was completed.

"End Test 1."

"Note end of Test 1." Micheal issued the command to print the random scribbles which conveyed the artistic mastery of a four-year old, a crayon, and a blank piece of paper.

"Test 2: Only move left leg from the knee." The first test was just to see if everything worked. This one isolated what they considered would be a basic signal for measuring a single range of motion.

"Test 2 started," Mark announced. It was clear that the device picked up on talking signals as the oscilloscope readout stuttered.

"Pause," Micheal halted the test. "We need to account for the talking in the experiment. Mark, can we count you down?"

"Yep. I will announce when I am ready and you count down to the start."

"Test 2 Ready," Mark initiated.

"3-2-1-Go," Micheal echoed.

Mark tried all he could to raise his leg, but nothing happened to his body. The scope, however, started recording single specific signals.

"Are you just trying to raise it, or are you trying to go up and down?" Micheal asked while looking to the screen and not knowing the range of signal he was looking at.

The oscilloscope wavered as Mark answered, "Just going up." Of course that introduced extra fuzz into the signals, so they dumped Test 2 and restarted again clarifying which signals were just up (Test 2a) and which were just down (Test 2b) and some were up then down (Test 2ab).

Four tests later, the data was dumped onto the server and sent to Mark's and Micheal's computers. David retreated to his office and the two young researchers returned to their corner of the lab to pass an attempt at making sense of the signals. They decided the best approach was to look at the data independently at first and then compare notes. It was tedious work trying to figure out the patterns in the signals. It took the rest of the day; several times of looking at the signals independently, and then together, then back to their own before the first pattern emerged.

"I think I see it," Micheal finally announced. Mark turned around to look at the highlighted section on his screen. It was a clear repeat, though the code was a little dirty.

"Do you think we can collect just those patterns and throw out the rest?" Micheal asked.

"Probably. It would be like using a speech to text filter. We need to look for the patterns and map them to the software while seeing everything else as garbage code to ignore."

"Well, that took all day. What next?" Micheal looked at his fated friend and lab partner.

"It is about time to go, so let's dump the rest of these on the server and I will stare at the other patterns and hopefully we will find more of them later. I think we need to look for the pattern in 2b and then see if we can identify both patterns alternating in 2ab."

"Yes, I think that is the best approach. Tomorrow afternoon, if we have these patterns, we will collect a few more to look at as homework but use most of the lab time figuring out how to put these signals to limbs," Micheal offered as a plan.

Susan arrived just when the researchers finished their plans for the data that was being uploaded to the laboratory server.

"How was your day?" Susan asked, waiting to interrupt their discussions.

"Good. I think we actually have progress!"

"Are you ready?"

Mark looked over to the computer to see the data was sitting at 92%. "Almost. We just need to wait for this upload, and then we can go."

The final few files were uploaded and Mark returned the computer to the login screen. The first day back to the lab was complete, and Mark had a strong sense of hope related to the possibilities this project could mean for himself and other people who find themselves in similar precarious positions.

Ӂ

Too many ideas rushed through Mark's mind to wait for the next day, so right after dinner he skipped television programs to start looking at the signals. He pulled up pattern 2b and stared at it for a while, but he kept looking for the 2a pattern in it. "Fresh eyes would help," the speaker echoed his own words back to him. He reasoned since he had another day of working on analyzing the signals, the morning would be a good time to look for the next pattern.

"Let's get this code working on a program." He found he liked talking to himself; it was a different voice than he was used to hearing back to himself, but his own words all the same, mirroring his inflections.

He pulled up a new text document and started with some basic code to start a simple application to respond to signals. Mark started with the output code of a true student of computer programming:

Hello World

Now to wrap it into a conditional: IF ELSE statements? Or should this be a FOR LOOP? He settled on the FOR LOOP because he reasoned the type of code did not matter, just the sequence of the input, but the FOR LOOP was faster to create. He opened up the pattern document and also the gibberish from Test 1. Grabbing the pattern code he dropped it into the condition test on the loop and fed the same pattern back to itself:

Hello World

That worked, but now, he had to test with dirty signals, so he fed the Test 1 output into the program:

Hello World

"Success," he told his empty room.

His code printed out the sequence. Obviously at some point in the random motion test he would have attempted to lift his leg. He copied the Test 1 code to a new document and pasted in three more instances of the pattern from Test 2a into it at various points and ran the code through the application:

Hello WorldHello WorldHello WorldHello World

The output reminded him that he always forgot the line breaks. But the code found the pattern and spit out the command. The code for sending specific signals to robotic limbs was at the lab and this small part satisfied his desires for now. He uploaded the simple application and logged out of the computer for the night.

The door to the programmer's office was dark as usual after the rest of the programmers left the junior team member to work on the final task. He stared at log files spitting data onto the screen, analyzing the results and looking for traces of the forbidden hardware. He was slowly sipping at a 20 ounce bottle of orange soda he had been nursing since the rest of the programmers departed. The door burst open startling him off his screen and into a rapid flinch to attention.

The older manager was staring down his young colleague. "What were the results of the latest tests? I want to give this device to Tyler, but we can't have any missteps here!"

The junior team member looked up sheepishly, "I'm looking over the logs now, sir. I am seeing exactly what you wanted. We are seeing the hardware we want to show, but not the hardware logging for the input devices."

"And there are no copies of the software drivers anywhere?" The boss asked, lightening his intimidating demeanor.

"No. Just the one you have."

"Great. I have looked over the files and made a few 'necessary' adjustments. I need you to set a cron job on your computer to push these to the server tomorrow morning during the work day, then the cron should self-destruct. Oh, and leave a copy of these files on your computer."

"OK, sir," the young programmer confirmed his understanding, "I'll get it done now."

"And where are the compiled drivers for the new device?"

"Right here," The young programmer grabbed a green USB drive from the desk. He studied it closely. "All the drivers and the installation instructions are here. I do have extra copies of this on the computer. Should those be erased?"

"No, as long as they are compiled so the code cannot be deciphered, I want them left behind. Finish up that cron job and go on home. I think we are good for the next phase of the project."

The door slammed closed again leaving the young programmer sighing in relief to be alone.

14

Mark's anticipation of working on the patterns woke him up before the sun shone on his face.

"Synaptergate: What time is it?"

"The current local time is 7:30 AM. Do you want the weather forecast?"

"Sure."

"Today is cloudy with a high near sixty-five. Ten percent chance of afternoon precipitation."

Mark was so happy he fiddled with the settings to give local times and English Units for the weather readout. He thought for a bit about his next project steps but realized he could not do much more than look for the patterns in the code.

"Time to get up!" He called. Nothing. Mark listened for noises in the living rooms. No television or pattern turning could be heard.

"Mom must not be up yet," he said to his silent room.

While she was a morning person, she often kept to herself in her bedroom for an hour after Eric left for work.

He called out again, but nothing. He scanned the room as best he could in his state. His eyes caught the old filing cabinet with the lamp on top and saw the buzzer. Since the speaker had been working so well, it was moved off the bed and placed uselessly on a cabinet. No one thought about an emergency restroom trip in the middle of the night, or they assumed the speaker could be heard.

During those long minutes Mark re-acquired the depression of the last six months as he realized he was totally stuck in bed until someone came for him.

"Where he she?" He yelled through the speaker to the lonely room. Now he was getting frustrated, but had nothing to do with his anger. He finally did the only thing he was able to: he cried in his cursed limitations. His mind went back to the frustrations of being paralyzed, his inability to talk, and his lack of desire to live.

With nothing left to do but wait, he was sucked into his memories and dozed back off to sleep.

"What do you think of Miss Loomis?" Mark said as the two childhood friends, now late teens, walked down the path through the woods between their houses.

Tim snorted and laughed, "You mean, besides the obvious?"

Miss Loomis was the new English teacher, not just new to the school, but a recent graduate of the local university.

Mark had seen her around the English department when he arrived at the writing center for the mandatory freshman tutoring in English 101. Her senior project oversaw the tutoring program which gave her more experience in teaching in her specialty field of English education.

Now at the high school and just out of college, Miss Loomis's class had the lowest sleeping rate in the high school among the male population. While her engagement as a teacher was excellent, the boys were more captured by her beauty and youth.

Mark looked at him and let out a giant laugh, "Actually, I was thinking of the obvious! You can't discount voluptuousness being displayed in the prime of youth!"

"Yeah," Tim let out with the tone of mental drool. "But really, she is the best teacher at the school...once you get focused on the material!"

Mark tried to hold back the grin, but was unable, "Yes, English class never held my attention so well. Of course, I used to see her at the college, too."

"You're kidding me! Where?" Tim insisted on knowing.

"Tutoring. We were required to go to the writing center for English 101, and she oversaw the program."

"You lucky dog! Did you ever talk with her...college student to college student?"

"Not really," he said trying to sound disinterested. "She was not a tutor; she just had her office in the tutoring room." He paused for a second, "How would you rate her?" He pulled in a deep breath and jumped over the little creek carving a path through the trail.

Tim took his leap, "Well," he said landing with firm, practiced footing, "I rate her well! Even for an adult!"

"Yeah," Mark agreed, "Mr. Mckeown?"

"Definitely not as cute!" Tim exclaimed.

Mark let out another uncontrollable laugh, "Ewww! As a TEACHER!"

"Well, we started talking about the cutest teacher in school! Why did you go from that to...ugh..." Tim and Mark caught each other's eyes and laughed again.

"Seriously, as a teacher?" Mark asked again.

"He's a decent teacher, nice, but never accepts late homework," said Tim.

"Well, do your work on time, dufus!"

"I'm just not a showoff like you are, Mark!"

"I know, I know," He paused to think of his next insult, "I'll just beat you on the scoreboard today, that will show me to be a real showoff!"

The boys reached the edge of the woods and ran up to the back porch still hurling good-natured insults toward one another.

Mark jolted back awake, the dream still fresh on his mind. He kept replaying the memory over and over. It was the last time Tim and Mark walked through the woods; the first conversation they shared on the last day they ever spoke. Mark then reflected on his first day back from the hospital in late November. It was the most frustrating day of his life. Sure, the days of being an infant were probably just as bad, but the loss of independence is always worse than if we never had it to begin with.

His once rich oral communications between family and friends became a belabored "YES" and "NO." What was the ACAT's first word other than those cursed words? "TV" it must have been; the abbreviated name for that box he mostly avoided in the past, but now had become infinitely more familiar with because it numbed his mind to his reality for long periods at a time. In the morning after baby food, "TV" right after lunch, "TV", the walks were not bad, but he could not say much; he did not want to. His parents tried to engage him, but eventually they stopped trying because he would not say anything more than simple one word answers. They all grew tired of hearing the computerized "YES" and "NO," so all communication ground to a halt.

His friends stopped coming by, not because they stopped liking him, but because they had no real expression in their friendships anymore. Relationship among kids is less about needs and more about laughter and casual insults. The fast-paced witty humor was destroyed by the belabored effort to speak with ACAT. Tim dropped off first, being most hurt by the loss of his friend. After all, how could they enjoy each other's company when the whole framework of their life had been climbing trees, walking to the local corner store, running through the woods, and playing video games? They mustered up a movie here or there, but the effect was not same when the laughs about the plot lines were all one sided, and Mark no longer contributed his analysis.

Micheal hung on a little longer. He would make the trip over from the college and tell Mark about the lessons he missed, and show him new schematics. Mark would do his best to talk, but conversations dropped off over the Christmas break, and he never regained the habit to come over during the spring semester.

The last six months were the hardest of Mark's life because he watched every friend disappear. Even his family's role in his life transformed from support roles to nurse maids. He resented what his life became as he was left to himself, Orion, and the television set. He had to break free and with all the emotion he could muster, he yelled out again.

"MOM!" He finally yelled at the top of the speaker's volume. Loud footprints rushed down the stairs and the door flew open, "What's wrong?" Said Susan, catching her breath.

"Time to get up," said Mark, casually.

"Mark, I thought you were in trouble! Why did you yell like that!" She paused for a second looking at Mark lifelessly laying there, unable to move anything more than a finger and his head. The silence lasted forever.

"Sorry," she finally whispered, forgetting he could not do the very things she had always taken for granted: just get up.

Mark was still not sure what to say. Sorry for yelling, or rebuking for not being there, or maybe something in between. No words needed to be said. They both knew getting him back to work would be the best answer.

"Let's get you up, then," Susan said with an apologetic tone.

"Thanks. Maybe we need to start putting the button back on the bed."

They both knew the button was like a text message. It conveyed a communication, but not the heart behind it. There was no voice fluctuation to make it sound like an emergency, but the mere ring of the bell would display an importance in responding. At least it was heard equally well in all parts of the house, but the speaker was just a voice in his room.

15

"I think I cracked the other patterns, Micheal." Micheal did not hear Mark's chair motor its way around the lab divider.

"Oh, hi," Micheal said, turning his eyes from the papers he was working on. He continued, "good. I looked at them, but had a big assignment to do, so I was not able to crack it. I am looking for it now."

"OK. I'll wait to see what you find, so we have confirmation. I have a few more things I can do here," he paused before adding, "Where are those robotic leg code snippets?"

"On the server. In the folder called 'snippets?'" He answered with a hint of snobbish sarcasm.

"Duh," Mark said, "I should have checked there first."

They both had their assignments and worked back to back, the silence only being pierced by Micheal flipping pages and hitting the occasional key on the computer. Mark, on the other hand, worked in total silence. His HID did not make even the quiet clanks or the click-clack of the keyboard.

"Got it," Micheal finally announced. Mark turned around and looked for the pattern that was now very familiar to him. They had confirmation moving the project into the next phase.

While Micheal looked over the pattern, Mark dropped code snippets for a mechanical leg into his bare bones application he had written the night before. The printer spun up and spit out a diagram he built for feeding the data into the arm.

"Can you grab that schematic?"

"What, are your arms broken?"

They both laughed at the absurd use of the playfully-rebellious sentiment.

Mark paused enough for his own pithy reply, "Well, no, but my primary motor cortex is...is that a valid excuse?"

"I guess so," He looked over the computer layout studying the pieces they would need, "Robert, are you busy?" He finally called out to the only other person in the lab.

A young Asian kid appeared from around the lab divider where Mark's old desk was situated. He looked to only be a year or so older than Mark. Robert's eyes looked over the scrawny, wheelchair bound kid before approaching nervously with his hand extended. "I'm Xin, but please call me Robert."

"Hi, Robert. I'm Mark."

He put his hand down, not quite sure what to think when no lips moved but the salutation came from behind his head.

"Meet Patient Zero, otherwise known as Mark."

"Pleased to meet you, sir!"

"Mark doesn't have any use of his hands, but needs something built. Do you have time before class to put this together?" He handed Robert the schematics for a computer board with a simple mechanical leg hanging off the side like some strange Frankensteinian test protocol.

Page after page turned in silence, then Robert looked up, "Yep. Pretty easy."

"Cool. You can do it right here if you want. Use the parts on the bench behind you. We'll be over at the computer in the corner if you need any clarifications," Micheal said.

Mark and Micheal headed to the other end of the room where the computer and oscilloscope were both setup to collect the implant readings. Now that they knew how to use the systems, David did not need to be around, so the two walked through more data collection. By the end of the day, they collected the less intricate long range motion of the elbows, knees, hips, and back movement. The data was fed to their computers and then dumped on the server.

They headed back to their desks to check in on Robert who was soldering on the final components.

"It's done, check it over," Robert offered the part to Mark forgetting he could not reach out and take it.

Micheal intercepted the circuit board and looked it over and then comparing the circuits to Mark's printout. "Looks good to me," he finally said while placing it on Mark's bench for his friend to examine.

Mark glanced over the board inspecting the top to his satisfaction.

"Flip it over," he ordered. Micheal neglected to examine the bottom of the board, but Mark knew from talking to Sam that both sides of the board should always be inspected. It was a good practice as one of the soldering balls was bridging a circuit which would have shorted the board.

"Looks like we have a cross in these circuits," Mark said, opening the plans and highlighting the circuit on the computer screen.

Robert grabbed the board for the final repair, and then when they were all pleased with the work, they got it ready to connect to the computer.

"Should we get David?" Mark questioned before feeding the program to the component.

"Sure, I think that would be good," said Micheal.

"I'm heading out to class now, so I'll let him know to come in." Robert picked up his bag from the bench around the corner and alerted David his presence was needed in the lab.

In just a moment, the professor walked in and casually sat in a lab stool, "Thanks for disrupting the paperwork, boys," He started, "what are we looking at?"

Micheal handed him a bundle of reports showing the patterns in the signals, the simple test program, the board schematics, and finally setting the board on the desk. It took about five minutes of flipping through everything before he picked up the board and inspected the work. Both the researchers watched him as the facial expressions cycle through various phases of curious, pleased, and excited.

"Let's try this thing out," he finally said. They connected the port on the board to the computer and Mark issued the command to send the test data feed into the box. The small robotic leg attached to the side of the module kicked out every time the signal was sent. An ecstatic response was elicited by the researchers. This was the first time signals from the implant were able to cause a predicable response.

"I need to call Tyler," the professor exclaimed, "This is incredible!"

"I want to test hooking up the signal recorder directly to the board. Can we try that?" Mark suggested.

"Grab the camera and get it set up. I'll call Tyler and see if he wants to make it over for this," David said.

Micheal retrieved the lab camera to record the results while Mark headed over to the computer with the signal collector and oscilloscope to await David's return. The board was connected to the computer, but they waited for Micheal to return and set up the camera. David had put some thought into how this would go already, so he explained the protocol to the researchers before rolling the footage. Mark was to wait for David to tell him what to move. The arm, back, head, legs. Mark would then move those parts and hopefully the leg component would be the only part to move when the leg command was issued.

The camera was set and the protocol was explained again for the camera. The experiment started.

"Arm," and the little robotic leg did not move.

"Leg," and motion was detected.

"Head," and Mark's head moved but the robot did not.

"Back," and the robotic arm was motionless.

"Foot," and the limb unexpectedly jerked.

"Leg," and the predictable motion was detected.

The experiment ended leaving the researchers in awe of the technology. The 'Foot' command was not as expected, but everything else worked perfectly.

Micheal was puzzled over the data, so he said to the team, "I think we need to collect a full range of leg to foot motions to figure out what is causing the robotic limb to jolt."

They all agreed, so Micheal setup the oscilloscope to view output, and David launched the data collection application. They fed different thoughts and signals into the machine and collected an excessive amount of data to dump on the server, plenty to keep the lab kids off the street for a few days.

The results led to a celebratory mood, so David suggested a trip down to the campus café to celebrate with some milkshakes…the one food they could all equally enjoy together.

They approached the little dining annex and were greeted by Tyler who was anxiously waiting for their arrival, so he could view the footage.

The shakes were ordered and the group sat down at the nearby table. Mark sucked down some of his chocolate milkshake while Micheal opened up the case to his tablet. They played the video of the lab test for Tyler, who watched it in excitement that they were able to quickly create a small robotic circuit that would respond to a specific signal from the implant. The celebration was well merited and the four discussed the next steps for their research.

The first goal was to figure out why the foot movements also triggered the leg movements, but no other command called the action. They conjectured the issue was a cascade event; moving the foot always moved the leg muscles in some way, so a command to move a hand or a finger might likewise move an arm.

"Do we need to create a robotic leg that mimics the actual body?" Tyler suggested as a discussion point.

If they needed to do that, the project would become extremely intensive, not to mention cyborg limbs might be required to fully function. Finally, it was suggested they try to map out commands that were more general, or see how walking might specifically compare to just moving a leg. If those could be mapped out, they thought reverse-engineering existing robotics and reorganizing code might be the most expedient approach. They had their plan including going back to the lab to record the motion of walking and how that related to isolated movements.

As they were getting ready to head back to the lab, Tyler reached into his pocket for some more drives. "I have another decoder here for you, Mark. And this green USB drive contains the drivers and instructions for the new device; it uses different drivers than the other one, being a different model in all. You can take this one home and set it up to do some small experiments at home if you want. We have another one in production that should be ready in a couple days."

He handed the implements to David and looked at his watch. "Well, Mr. Jones will want an update, so I need to head back to the office."

"Later, Tyler. Thanks for the milkshakes and the hardware!" Mark told him on the way out.

16

Tyler opened the door to the office and walked over to the desk. He sat in his swiveling chair and stretched his hands up in a yawn just when his phone beeped. Letting out a sigh, he reached for the phone to remember what the notification was about.

"How could I forget?" He yelled to himself quickly grabbing his soft leather briefcase he just set on the floor. He rummaged quickly through the bag looking for a few personal effects including headphones, his wallet, and car keys, throwing them onto the desk as he ran out the door.

Thoughts raced through his mind while the elevator crawled its way to the penthouse floor of the office building. The last time he was summoned to the executive conference room was back in January when he was promoted to the project manager position. He was appointed after Mr. Jones found out he had connections to the local renowned robotics professor and that one of his students had been seriously injured. Tyler was able to get the professor and the family on board for a revolutionary new project that would help anyone in Mark's unfortunate circumstances.

"Hello, Mr. Davis," Mr. Jones said when Tyler walked into the room. "Have a seat. The single agenda in this meeting is the progress on Patient Zero."

Tyler glanced around the room. He knew Mr. Jones and Mr. Meyer, but only recognized the chairman of the board from photographs.

"Let's get started," Mr. Jones said blandly as he closed the door. "Tyler, have you met our chairman?"

"No, sir," he said to Mr. Jones. He continued, turning this time toward the chairman, "It is a pleasure to meet you, Mr. Chairman."

He admired the Chairman's Brook's Brother's suit, examining how all the pieces were perfectly tailored to his muscular body tone. The deep voice cracked the corners of the room.

"Thank you, son. Mr. Jones has been telling me you are the right man for this job. I can't wait to see our progress. This could be the most significant help computer technology has ever brought to medical science."

"I am glad to be part of such an important research project, sir." He nodded and looked once more around the room and suddenly felt uncomfortable in the presence of the most prestigious men in the company.

"Well, let's get to this," the chairman started, "I read over the reports from the hospital. It looks like the implant was successfully inserted and all the wounds are healed up. We have not received the final CT scan yet, but

Dr. Jacobs informed Mr. Meyer that the scan will be delivered to him today."

"Yes, Mr. Chairman," Mr. Meyer interjected, "He assured me the scans would be in today at 5:00, so he'll be staying late at the hospital until they arrive. We are meeting first thing in the morning to receive those scans."

"Excellent," the chairman said. Turning once again to Tyler, "What's the status of Patient Zero?"

"Thank you, Mr. Chairman. I just came from a meeting with the whole research team at the university. We have some video that I was able to view, but it was too fresh to get a copy. They probably have it uploaded to the server by now, but I have the original reports right here."

Tyler shuffled through documents in his briefcase finally bringing forth the stack of papers from the lab. It contained the raw data outputs, patterns, code, and board specs.

"I just arrived from the lab and did not have time to make copies, but here is the initial report."

Mr. Jones cut him off, "Debbie?" He rang his secretary through the intercom. The door opened, "Yes, sir?"

"Can you make a copy of this for everyone and one extra for the file? Also, check the research server for the university files to see if they recently uploaded a video. If so, please queue that for us to view."

"Right away, sir," and she closed the door again.

"Please continue, Mr. Davis."

"Thank you. In the video I saw, the implant decoder was connected to the device in the blueprints. When Ma… Patient Zero was instructed to move certain limbs, only the leg and foot responded. They are working out a few bugs, but otherwise the mechanical limb is moving as expected. They have a few plans to work out the issue and will update me as soon as that occurs."

"Thank you, Mr. Davis. We'll review the video if they have it uploaded." Turning this time to Mr. Meyer, "What do you have to report?"

"We had some issues with what we think is signal reverberation, but after some new programming that seems to have been resolved. We passed the new device and the drivers to Mr. Davis." After a brief pause he redirected back to the new manager, "Did you deliver the decoder and drivers?"

"Yes, Mr. Meyer. It was delivered today when I was at the university. I told Patient Zero to take take them home because the second decoder will be delivered to the lab shortly."

"Any negative effects?"

"Nothing has been reported to me, Mr. Meyer. I'll update you personally if I hear of anything."

"Thank you," he responded to Mr. Davis, then he continued, "Our next step is to start viewing the data being collected by the decoders. We should be able to see the signals, and the speaker will give us a little insight into what is being tried and why."

"What do you mean?" Tyler asked apprehensively.

"You don't need to worry about that part," Mr. Jones stated blankly, "Mr. Meyer's looking for any anomalies with his auditing team."

"I thought Patient Zero's lab was the only one working on the project directly."

"He is, but we need to have a hands on lab and one that is disconnected from the situation, so we can monitor for any side effects. This was always in the project plan," Mr. Meyer countered, "You don't need to concern yourself with it. And Mr. Davis, the other lab can't know about our monitoring of the situation. That could negatively skew our results. Is that understood?"

The board room fell silent for a moment. "Is that understood, Mr. Davis?" Mr. Jones echoed.

"Ye- yes, sir. I understand," Tyler said sheepishly.

The room felt tense, but these gentlemen knew how to calm such situations. "This is to help Mark the best we can. We do not want the project enthusiasm to let things get out of hand. Taking things too far could be a detriment. Besides, our insurance company always required this extra step. This is all in the documents. That makes sense, doesn't it?" Mr Jones added.

"Of course, sir," Tyler finally said. Still, uneasy about this plan, but not wanting to display apprehension to these businessmen more experienced than himself.

The presentation screen caught them all off guard as a video was loaded up and paused at the beginning. The door opened at once and Debbie had four packets and a remote in her hand. She passed out the reports and handed the remote to Mr. Jones. "You're all set, sir."

"Thank you, Debbie. I think that's all we need for now, so you can take your lunch if you want."

"Thank you, sir." She voiced pleasingly while closing the door again.

"Mr. Davis, what're we looking at?" Mr. Jones directed again to Tyler.

He flipped quickly through each page of the packet before turning back to the first page.

"On page one, we have the basic protocols they are using. To summarize, they are feeding known commands into the recorder and then analyzing the patterns to find out how to call certain actions. Any questions there?"

The three businessmen looked at each other and the pages, "No, please go on," the Chairman ordered.

"The next few pages is the raw, simplified code for how the implant signals are being converted into robotic limb signals. And the final pages are the raw board schematics."

"Excellent. Let's have a look at this video."

Mr. Jones clicked on the play button and the executives watched how the research team was able to cause a little leg attached to a computer board to kick when the subject thought about moving his leg. They were astounded at the quick progress and excited to see their device was paying off.

"Mr. Meyer, any comments?"

"Mr. Chairman, it would appear we're actually a little ahead of schedule. I am pleased to see this much progress." He paused for a moment before redirecting back to Tyler, "Mr. Davis, excellent work. Keep that team happy and the progress videos coming. And please do let me know personally if anything strange is reported."

"Thank you, Mr. Meyer, I will."

"Let's stay on top of this and not rest on our laurels for being ahead of schedule. Good work everyone, I guess we're done. Thank you, Mr. Davis, Mr. Meyer."

The two junior managers left the room, leaving Mr. Jones and the chairman by themselves.

PART 3:
SOMETHING AMISS

17

"How long before dinner?" Mark asked while pushing his way up the ramp into the house.

"Probably about an hour. Dad'll be home soon, so we'll walk first."

"OK. Can you plug a drive into the computer for me?"

Mark told her where to locate the new device and accompanying drivers. Mark used his words to explain where to put the flash drive. To him it was obvious, but to a complete computer ignoramus like Susan, it was a difficult task to find the perfectly sized port among the other ports on the front of the computer.

"No down more."

"This one?"

"No, more," The frustration in his voice was just starting to crackle through.

"This one?"

"Too far. Up a bit," Now he was convinced she was just messing with him, though she was not.

"Here?"

"Perfect!"

The drive was in.

"OK, now the other one goes into any port on the back of the computer that looks just like this one," he was hoping she would make the distinction between a USB port and a HDMI port, but she got it in there.

"It is in. If you need anything else…please wait for your father! I'm starting dinner," Susan scolded.

The data on the device included another vague computer-lingo text-to-PDF which Mark copied to the folder on his computer. It also included an application that was already compiled labeled as 'decoder-driver-cc' which he also moved. The software was designed to interface with the new USB device like the lab version. The Man Page indicated this one would not allow the collection of data but simply output the data from the decoder directly into the control board. This was the first prototype for the commercial, non-research version of the hardware. He studied the documents and found the methods to interface it through the computer, directly through the board, or by making connections through the speaker; the latter being the least cumbersome option because it allowed the single receiver to connect multiple devices at once. This required him to attach a small networking board to each device. The instructions to flash his specific chip were included, so no two people with an implant could operate the same device.

"Mark, are you ready to take a walk?" Eric interrupted. Mark was too focused on reading that he did not hear his dad enter the house.

"Sure. Let me start pulling data from the server first so it has a chance to download." And he turned to the computer causing drives to open, data to appear on the screen, and a transferring notification in the upper corner of the window. "Ready."

Eric was impressed with the speed with which Mark was able to accomplish the task on the computer. He was expecting a five or ten minute wait, but the command was executed in a matter of seconds. They both left the room and headed outside, down the end of the street, right on Pineview and toward the park. The leaves were starting to display their full splendor as if unfurling to Mark's own progress.

"How's the research going?" Eric had not heard any of the news yet, but neither had Susan.

"Good. We were already able to cause a robotic leg to move when I want it to. We need to figure out a bug, though."

Mark explained the bug as the lab saw it: random limb movements had no effect on the leg movement, but the foot move did cause the leg to move.

"Hmm..." After the explanation of the problem, Eric offered some ideas based off his knowledge of anatomy. "It would seem to be that the reason the foot motions trigger something in the leg is that some muscles cascade in their movements. Thinking of the anatomy of the leg, the foot rotation is not completely decoupled from the calf, but a toe, for example is. So try to test just toe motions, I bet they will not trigger the leg."

"So would a robotic leg need toes to walk?" Asked Mark.

"It might if it's using signals from your head but maybe not if you find walking-specific code and map that to a foot. Sam might know the answer to that."

They continued talking about various protocols, anatomy of bones and muscles, and how they might be able to get arms, legs, and bodies working with their mind. Susan was lost in the conversation, but was happy to see some sense of normality returning between father and son. It seemed almost like old times again.

"Wawawawa, Wawawawa, Wawawawa," Susan's phone suddenly broke the silence of a pause in conversation.

"Hello?" The voice was familiar and a little frantic, "it's for you honey. John."

"John, what's up?" "Really?" "Yes, just after dinner is fine." "See you then."

Susan and Mark were left to guess at the subject of the conversation, only able to hear half of it. It was unusual for John to call Susan's phone, and certainly not very common for him to stop by in the evening without prior planning.

"What is up?" Mark finally inquired.

"John said there's something in the CT scan I need to see, and he didn't want it to wait until morning."

"Should we be concerned?" Susan stuttered.

"Not sure. We'll know tonight."

Ӂ

John's mysterious phone call cast off the usual jovial mood surrounding the dinner table, causing everyone to eat in relative silence. Mark mostly stared at his picture in the family portrait, the very thing that usually stole his focus from other matters.

"Does anything hurt, Mark?" Susan's words broke his concentration on his past able-bodied life, "What?"

"Does anything hurt?" She repeated.

"No. Why?"

"I was just wondering if John sees something that might cause pain."

"Oh. No, nothing like that."

He fixed his eyes again on the picture, studying his old beige sweater, trying not to focus on the mush being fed to him at Susan's will.

"Do you have any strange thoughts?" She interrupted his thoughts again.

Mark looked to his dad to see if he was reacting.

"Mark?" Susan asked again.

"What?!" He snapped.

"Do you have any strange thoughts?"

"Mom! I will tell you if anything is out of place!" He finally yelled back.

"Don't yell at me! I am just making sure you are OK!"

"Sorry," he lowered his demeanor, "I will let people know if I need anything. Until then, can we just wait for John. He may not have anything to say at all."

"Just calm down everyone," Eric finally burst out sensing the odd dinner time that starkly contrasted the amazing conversation during the walk to the park.

"I am calm," Mark forced, "I am just thinking about our next steps for the project."

The awkward meal crawled to a halt and Susan started cleaning dishes when the doorbell rang. Eric promptly opened the door for John, who was clutching a card case that could have contained either a large map or a fishing pole.

"Thanks for making time tonight. I wanted to show you this, but the guys at Synaptergy have asked for all copies of the medical documents to be sealed because they're funding the research, including the medical expenses," said John, walking into the house.

"I assume that's the CT scan?" Eric said.

"Yes."

"Alright, lets go to the garage."

The garage was the only room in the house with large overhead lights that would make viewing a scan easy enough for a pair of doctors to view together. They cleared off space on the workbench and pulled the shop light off the chain, laying it down with the bulbs pointing from the bench. The makeshift back light illuminated the motor cortex region. Without any help, Eric spotted the issue straight away: the implant looked like a cluster of octopuses wrapping around various parts of the brain.

"What do you think?" Eric finally asked; John was the more accomplished neurosurgeon of the two.

"Well, as long as there are no effects or pain, and the thing is done spreading out tentacles, it is OK, but this thing can never be removed. The damage would be too catastrophic to consider extracting it all. In other words, if the experiment works, that's great, but if it doesn't, he will be like a gunshot survivor with a bullet lodged forever in his body, only this bullet is technologically active!"

"So ultimately, even if the experiment is a failure, he's stuck with this forever?" Asked Eric.

"Correct. They're going to want this scan, and they were pretty clear they did not want anyone to know about this copy, so keep it under wraps. I want to do another scan in a few weeks to see if it is done expanding or not. I'll make that official call tomorrow afternoon after I drop this scan off at Synaptergy." John was outlining a plan in his head.

Eric went into the house to feign using the restroom, but he really grabbed the small camera in his bedroom, sliding it into his pocket.

"Can you make some tea, honey?" He said in passing through the kitchen on the way back to John who remained in the garage. They snapped some photos of the scan and hid the SD card among the mess of tools in the garage. They didn't want anyone else knowing about the photo or the results. With that, they wrapped up the scan, fixed the workbench, and headed in for a bit of light socializing.

"What's the problem?" Susan asked when John sat down at the table to a cup of hot tea.

"No problem. I just got that scan in today, but the guys at Synaptergy want it in the morning, so I brought it over to let Eric have a look at it before the meeting first thing. I'm going over it with their medical team in the morning, but I'll have the official news tomorrow. I'll call you then with the updates after our meetings."

Eric understood the story immediately and kept replaying it in his mind, so he did not tip their hand about anything else.

"What does it look like, can I see?" Mark asked.

"I already wrapped it back up. It is just a scan with a little implant on it. I'll get you a copy tomorrow if I can." He already realized that was not going to be specifically possible, but it stopped the progression of the conversation at present. He knew he needed to change the topic, so he offered to hear about the current research, instead.

After some time of listening and hypothesizing with the other doctor in the room it was time to head out for the evening. "Thanks for the tea!" He offered as his exit line. Eric followed him back out to the car and exchanged a few more words out of earshot of the other two.

18

Just before 10:45, John Jacobs entered the Synaptergy building sporting a soft leather briefcase slung over his shoulder and a hard tube case containing the CT scan he showed Eric the previous night. He walked confidently toward the security desk in the center of the lobby just inside the swiveling doors.

"11:00 with Mr. Meyer, please." John announced to the security station attendant.

The security guard studied the appointment list for a moment, "Dr. Jacobs? Can I see some identification, please?"

The security was serious. It reminded John of the top secret work he had done in military contracts in his former days before settling down to raise a family. While the Synaptergy group was very secretive, most research was just as secure to prevent information leaks before the company was in position to allow such data into the public eye.

"Thank you, Dr. Jacobs. Do you know your way to his office?" The guard handed back the ID looking at him in the eye with a light smile.

"Yes," he confirmed, walking beyond the security station still fumbling to slip his driver's license back into his wallet with his hands full. He slipped the wallet back into his pocket and pushed the up button on the elevator. After a thirty-second ride up, the door dinged open and John stepped out into the hallway directly across from Mr. Meyer's office. He cleared his throat outside and then opened the door to the outer office.

"Mr. Meyer is expecting you, Dr. Jacobs," the secretary softly confirmed without looking up. John quietly closed the door, not wanting to disturb the eerie silence of the executive suites.

"Thank you, Mrs. Johnson," he said in passing, opening the door on the right leading into the inner office.

"Good morning, Dr. Jacobs," Mr. Meyer began. "Is that the scan?" Pointing to the case.

"Yes, sir, as requested."

"Excellent. Has anyone else seen it?" Mr. Meyer continued.

"No, just me. I received it late afternoon yesterday and took it home with me so no one on the night staff could peek at it," said John in a comforting tone.

"And what do you think?" Mr. Meyer said, tilting his head and eying the scan.

"Well, I want to run another scan. I am little concerned with the results here but I do not see any long term issues as long as the implant does not continue to expand."

"What do you mean?"

"Have a look here," he started to unfold the scans while walking toward the window to use it as a back light. "You can see here the implant. It has spread out with hundreds of tentacles into the patient's brain matter. As long as it is done growing, I don't see any issue, but this implant can never be removed."

"It's done growing. I'm sure of it," he said with confidence. "We've seen this behavior with the implant in the rats. The device grows only that much, but no more."

John asked anyway, "Can we do another scan, for my ease of mind?"

"I don't really think it's necessary, but if you want to, you can schedule another one. Same as before. You bring the scan directly to me, no one else looks at it, no other copies are made."

"And what do I show the family? His father is a doctor and will want to have a look at the scans for himself," John asked.

"We've thought of that. I have a scan here you can show him." Mr. Meyer reached into a cabinet behind him and grabbed a scan resembling the one John had brought in. This time, however, the doctored scan displayed what looked like the implant, but without any tentacles. "Show him this scan instead. It's also the official copy for the medical team meeting at the hospital."

John opened the scan and admired it at the window for a few minutes. "Do you think this will fool a doctor who has seen his son's scans from before we were ever involved?"

"Certainly. We based this one off his old scan. It is patient zero's initial scan with the implant edited into it. He can keep this one. It is a perfect duplicate without the tentacles. Understand, there is nothing wrong or dangerous about them, they just look freaky, and we think it'd be bad publicity that would overshadow what we are trying to do. As long as you think the tentacles will not impact Patient Zero's brain, we will proceed."

"Yes, I agree. Every other test came back clean. He has my full doctor's permission to do any amount of work he deems he's able to. He has instructions to report directly to me with any issues."

"Then we're good without that second scan, John?"

"Well, it's just this. Any protocol for this type of work would have multiple scans. It'd raise suspicions if we stopped at only one."

"OK," he paused and sighed, his eyes rolling to the top of his head to see his thoughts, "It was hard enough fixing the machine the first time to not leave digital copies," he paused to stroke his bare chin before continuing, "What if we run the scan here? We'll sell it as we need a second scan. You'll still be the interpreter, but we'll do it here to make sure the hospital scanner images do not leak."

John paused to think over the plan, "Yes, that'll work. Let's say in about two weeks?"

"Perfect, we'll schedule the scan here in the morning, and do a press release party with Patient Zero as the highlight in the afternoon."

John agreed, taking the doctored scans to present to the hospital team and the family while Mr. Meyer started the forms and calls to schedule the party.

Ӂ

At the university, Mark presented the experiments his father suggested, and the results were just as predicted. This gave them the working theory that any muscle movement triggering a cascade of muscles would produce messy signals. That meant they needed to either create a robot with all the muscles as mechanical parts, or else single out patterns for isolated movements and integrate those into existing robotics theory.

"I see at least two downsides to creating a robot with full anatomical properties," David stated in the brainstorming session. "First, that's more complicated than robotics has ever been, so it'd take a lot of extra research to delicately create such limbs, though they would be far smoother than the alternative. Second, that'd likely increase our time to achieve the results we are looking for."

"There is a third," Mark chimed in. "That would also require cybernetics and cutting off limbs to return real function. I think an exosuit is our real answer, so we collect more complicated movements now, clean out the code with averages, and integrate that into our current technology. We can look at the more complicated approaches later if need be."

Science is built upon prior knowledge in smaller parts, so that made more sense than any other option, so it was the approach the lab adopted. The first task was going to be focusing on the arms to see if they could map in a range of functions. Lift up, set down, turn right, turn left. Such an approach would take more mastering and conscious effort, but at the same time, they could see results sooner while learning what it would take to refine the applications to each muscle instead.

With the planning out of the way, Mark decided it was time to plug the hardware device into the speaker. He explained the details and how the speaker could be used to control several devices at the same time. For the rest of the day, they worked on connecting the board to one of the data receivers, flashing the firmware for his chip onto the board they created, and attaching a little arm to the board to replace the leg. This would allow him to add specific code to the application to control the arm for simple tests any time.

Ӝ

In the afternoon after the Synaptergy meeting, John had an official meeting with Eric and the rest of the surgical team on the progress of Patient Zero. He presented the scan Mr. Meyer had given him as the report to include in the medical write up. The whole team took turns admiring the scans, conjecturing that everything looked perfect, and all giving their approval of success.

"Finally, mark your calendars for a press event. In two weeks to this day, Synaptergy will be hosting a press release and celebration. Both the surgical and research teams will present at the public meeting. As I understand, the research team has also made some incredible breakthroughs." Turning to Eric, he continued, "Also, they'll do the next round of scans at their headquarters that morning."

John adjourned the meeting, and the doctors, except for Eric, scattered to their other duties.

"Here's an extra copy of the scan for your family, Eric." He winked and cracked a smile. They never discussed the unofficial meeting, and it was too risky to do it at the hospital anyway.

Eric took the scan back to his locker to remember to bring it home. He now stood conflicted about whether to share the real details with Mark and Susan, or if he should just pass off the forgery as the original. Such questions haunted him for the rest of the day, but his mind was finally made up by the time his turn signal clicked off, and he was heading up his driveway. For now, the best thing to do is minimize concern but reinforce the original plan that Mark needs to call someone if he experienced any adverse feelings.

He confidently brought in the scan calling for Mark and Susan. Eric spread out the scan across the dining room window, pointing out the implant and various other parts of the brain like a kid showing off some new toy.

"What's this mean?" Susan finally said.

"Well, it means that the implant is inserted, and all the wounds are healed. Mark's fully clear for anything, medically speaking." Then he addressed Mark directly, "But you still need to let us know if you feel out of the ordinary, particularly in the head."

"I will. I think this is a good time to see if we have any way to control a cell phone with this device, that would help with logistics and other things as well as communicating any needs more rapidly."

The family was agreed about calling if trouble arose and wanting to connect a phone to the speaker if possible. Eric unfolded the plan about the meeting at Synaptergy and made sure the date was on the calendar. Mark was to tell David and the rest of the lab about it, though Tyler would probably reach out to him as well.

The family was convinced about the safety of the implant for now, and Eric had fully placed confidence in John that he knew what he was doing. John had worked on a lot of 'hush-hush' teams in the past, and the thought even crossed his mind that Eric hoped his friend was truly on his side...but he had to be, otherwise Eric would never have known about the other scan. Still, Eric kept thinking back to the images of the real scan that were hidden in the garage and wondering if this was the right decision, but he stood fast and thought ahead to the progress and Mark's possible future. He hid his conflict well, and carried about his usual routine with the family, or at the desk.

19

The next week of research brought mostly progress coupled with a few setbacks. Still, they were able to map out the functions needed to program an arm and Mark went to work developing the circuit board for the function. Once he had a segment prepared, Robert had his practice at assembling the components. A few days before the big Synaptergy party, they finally had an arm-sized robotic limb in the lab. They were ready for testing.

David took a chair by the arm, which the lab took to calling 'The Claw'. Micheal powered up the camera while Robert stood by watching his board circuitry be put to the test.

"This is the first test of The Claw," David said to the camera, "Data collected by Mark, A.K.A. Patient Zero, and Micheal. Boards assembled by Robert with project oversight by Professor David. This is the initial test of the full size arm. The micro-scale prototype has been documented previously."

The tests began. It was less of a scientific experiment and more of a party resembling preteen boys excited about how a smartphone works. Mark started with raising The Claw in the air like he was asking a question. The arm then lowered back down and held itself out poised, for a handshake from Robert. He obliged making a historic breakthrough for this technology. The grip was neither too lax nor too firm, but Mark could adjust his grip with the same fluidity he could when he had control over his body, though he lacked the biofeedback needed to know exactly how hard to squeeze.

He picked up a variety of objects with the same ambition that he had with his now useless arm. Finally, Mark asked for a glass of water to be placed on the desk. He hesitated, but finally picked up the glass and brought it to his lips. He had just enough control to make a partial seal over the cup; he was able to drink, but with a partial spill of water down the front of his shirt. Mark was never so excited to spill water on himself. But it was too much emotion for the moment.

He studied the glass being poised in the robotic arm being controlled by his mind and a small tear rolled down his cheek. He slowly set the glass down, turned his chair, and rolled out of the lab. Micheal followed behind him with the camera rolling, but David called out, "Let'm go, Micheal."

Mark went down to the elevator at the end of the hall, but had no ability to push any buttons to escape. He instead found an accessible corner to cry with a solemn mixture of joy and sorrow.

After a few minutes, he stopped crying and breathed out the rest of his emotion. He took an extra few minutes to compose himself fully and turned back to the lab. David was back in his office, so Mark rolled in there first.

"Sorry, Professor." He said quietly at the door.

"Come in, Mark," he answered, "It's OK. This is a powerful experiment for us, something the likes of we have never seen, but as powerful as it is for us, it's infinitely more so for you. We–me and Micheal–understand the challenges and difficulties. It'd be better if we had this project without your circumstance, but here we are."

"True, but without my circumstance we would not have this opportunity. We need to see this through. We need to finish this project, whatever the finish is," said Mark.

David collected his words carefully before continuing, "What's the finish for you, Mark?"

He hesitated, picking his words carefully, "To be able to walk, to be able to hold out my hand. I want the ability to move myself."

"Well, I think the idea of an exosuit is the best plan, but it comes with risk. If it does something we don't plan on, it'd crush you."

"I am willing to take that risk. I am nothing in this chair," Mark said boldly.

"Directly after the meeting we'll put our resources into it. In the meantime, lets go into the lab and see if we can attach that arm to your wheelchair."

They left the office and headed back to the lab. Micheal and Robert were already busy scribbling out ideas for how to attach the arm to Mark's chair. They had several clamps which they reasoned would work. They needed to attach the battery for the mechanical limb to a longer cable to make room for it somewhere in the basket on the chair.

Once David and Mark joined the crew they took an hour affixing the limb to the chair. The battery was run from the basket by the speaker and everything seemed to be looking correct.

"High five," Mark yelled. Micheal hit The Claw with his hand. Robert went for it when Mark jolted it out of the way, "Too slow!" He laughed.

Mark turned around to leave the lab again.

"Now where're you going?" Micheal yelled out.

"Just get the camera and follow me."

The crew approached the elevator, and The Claw shot out and pressed the button to go down. The doors opened and the lab team stepped inside, now minus David who stayed behind with the lab and some paperwork. Mark pressed the button for the first floor, and they waited for the doors to open back up.

The elevator door rumbled open and the lab team stepped out. Mark guided them down one corridor after another, Micheal still recording.

"Where are we going, Mark?" Robert called out in tow.

Mark was silent, but turned the final corner near the back door leading out of the building, but stopped before the exit. He turned a ninety-degree angle to the left, aligning his vision on a vending machine.

"Does anyone have a dollar?"

Robert pulled a dollar from his wallet and was about to put it into the machine when Mark stopped him.

"Put it in my bag, in the zipped pouch and close it all up again."

Micheal watched as Robert followed the instructions. After they stepped back, the limb grasped the zipper and opened the bag. The Claw grabbed the dollar, shook it out, and bent it longways so it would go into the machine. The primitive vending machine accepted the bill and the finger on the arm pushed D2. After a whirring of the rotating spiral, and the vending machine dropped a payload of Skittles into the retrieval bin. Mark commanded The Claw to go in after it. After some shifting of the chair and the arm, he hoisted his prize in front of his face, "Who wants some Skittles?"

The three researchers, behaving more like middle school boys playing mischievously, headed back to the elevator approaching it right about the time Susan was walking down the hall to pick up Mark.

"Quick," Mark yelled, "stand in front of the arm!"

Micheal knew what Mark was up to, so he hid the object from Susan's view.

"Mom!" He yelled out, "I have something for you!"

Susan quickened her pace, "What is it?" She said, finally in front of him.

The arm reached out between the lab mates, still holding the red package of skittles.

"Want a Skittle?"

Of course, the bag was still sealed, but Susan was aghast.

"Are you moving that arm?" She hesitated.

"Yep!" He said with an excited glow.

The Claw dropped the Skittles into his lap and reached out toward Susan's hand. He grabbed her hand gently. He could not feel her touch, but she let out her own sobs as she felt a hand controlled by her son for the first time in half a year.

She stepped back to examine how it was attached to the wheelchair; admiring the bolts, clamps, and wires.

"How does it work?" She asked.

They took turns explaining various details of the mechanics. She had no idea what any of them were talking about, but she did enjoy their enthusiasm.

"We need to stop by David's office," Mark finally said, picking the Skittles back up.

Mark approached the closed door, so he did the only natural thing: he knocked.

"Come in."

So the arm reached out and turned the doorknob. He pushed the door open and rolled in and placed the pack of Skittles on the pile of papers on David's desk, "Want a Skittle?"

"Where'd you get this?"

"The vending machine. You owe Robert a dollar."

"This is incredible. Did anything fail to work yet?" Said David.

"Nope, all seems well. I will give things a try tonight and see if anything needs adjustments."

And with that, the most accomplished lab day the team had yet experienced drew to an end.

20

Synaptergy headquarters bustled with activity. Balloons and banners decorated the air midway between the floor and the high ceiling to brighten the otherwise sanitized lobby. Caterers hosted the most glorious party, and at Mark's request, they had a milkshake vendor. In addition, various entertainers were brought in to work the room. Magicians, jugglers, and sketch artists made rounds throughout the crowd. No expense was spared to make this the event of the year.

On the far side of the room, a podium was erected and several technicians for various news anchors were setting up microphones to collect every word of the speeches that had not yet convened. Several reporters were walking around trying to read the attitudes in the room and collecting comments.

The company invited the research and medical teams, employees, board members, and investors. They also reached out to other doctors in the medical community hoping to garner more support for the project and find new test subjects for their product. Robotics and technology companies were also invited to create partnerships with other robotics laboratories and industries. Being the first public release of the product, Mr. Jones wanted to garner as much publicity out of this event he could. He was talking to reporters and investors, working the room to inform everyone of the amazing new technology.

Mark had arrived hours before the party began and demonstrated the use of the robotic arm to the Synaptergy board. He also went through some more medical tests with John at the company's private medical lab. They were finishing up the scans about the time the party guests started trickling in.

"We're about to begin, Mark," Jessica, Mr. Meyer's assistant said, interrupting the final tests.

"Thank you. Let us get going," said Mark.

They left the lab, making their way through corridors, as quiet as a mausoleum, following Mr. Meyer's assistant.

She led them out behind a curtain where the party was in full force.

"Please wait here. Mr. Jones would like to announce you with a speech," and she vanished into the crowd to inform the CEO they were ready.

"Ladies and gentlemen, if you will please find your seat we will begin shortly," Jessica said from the podium, watching over everyone like a sentient robot herself.

The press tables near the front of the room filled up quickly with a host of reporters, all fidgeting for voice recorders and notepads. Mark's parents and the research lab occupied the front and center reserved table.

"Thank you, Ms. Johnson," Mr Jones said from the podium, "Friends, associates, doctors, researchers, we're here today to announce the greatest breakthrough in medical robotics our world has ever seen. Hundreds of thousands of people find themselves paralyzed every year from accidents of various kinds. While formerly, those people would be forced to stay at home and give up their career passions, we have been making breakthroughs that will bring workers back to the marketplace! Today we want to introduce you to research that promises to help restore lost mobility in patients and give our society better efficiency at handling our current work."

"We have been working tirelessly for over three years to develop a new chip that allows its owner to control both simple, and complicated tasks just by thinking about them. This chip has already demonstrated the ability to use a computer up to ten times faster than traditional means, but even better, we will show you today that after only a month with this chip, our first test subject is now able to do something he has not be able to do for over seven months."

Mr. Jones paused his speech for a moment and glanced around the room.

"Before we introduce him, let's take a moment of silence. This young man lost the ability to move his body in ways we all take for granted. It was tragic, but through that tragedy was born the desire and motivation to break out of the depression of his loss, and move ahead into a bright new future."

His pause was just uncomfortable enough for the reporters to glance around the room for someone who might be the research subject the CEO referenced. The silence seemed planed, as if Mr. Jones was just waiting for the isolated cough from the back of the room before resuming, "It is my pleasure to introduce you to Mark, our very own Patient Zero!"

Mark rolled his chair from behind the curtain and up onto the stage. He approached Mr. Jones and reached his robotic arm out to shake the CEO's hand. The crowd applauded and looked in wonder while the various camera persons were tripping over one another for the best shot of the historic handshake.

"A month ago, ladies and gentlemen, Mark was unable to speak. To my understanding, he can now tell us his favorite drink, go and get it, and feed himself!" directly talking to Mark now, he said, "Go ahead and show us, son."

Mark rolled off the stage and over to the milkshake vendor. The speaker affixed to his chair called out, "One vanilla shake, please." The Claw reached out to receive the drink, and he rolled back up on stage to announce his milkshake. He lifted the shake to his mouth and began to drink.

The crowd burst into applause, but the front table looked at each other, slightly puzzled.

"Professor?" David was caught off guard. He had not realized he was called upon to talk about the project, but remembered when his name was called from the podium.

"Sorry," he recovered from his fumble of words when he took the stage, "We were still astonished by his ability even now!"

The crowd chuckled along with him.

"I first met Mark when he was thirteen years old at our summer robotics youth camp, though I must confess I didn't remember that detail until he told me about it later. He has been working in my lab for a few years, however, and he was always one of the most talented robotics students we have seen, especially since he was still in high school. But our little robotics projects turned into this huge undertaking, with the help of Synaptergy, to fix Mark when he lost all control over his body."

David continued, "I first learned of the project when my old college partner and roommate heard one of my students had become disabled. He was recently promoted to the head of research for the project, and he reached out to see if it was something we could work on together, like old times. I will leave the future plans for this implant for him to discuss, but today I want to tell you about how we were able to make all this work."

"It starts with an implant created by the Synaptergy engineers. The chip will intercept the signals from the primary motor cortex and send them out via a shortwave frequency. We were able to scientifically isolate the many patterns that make an arm move and map them to an electronic board that receives this data and sends the signals to the limb. Now that we know what causes all the patterns, Mark is able to will the limb to do what he wants, just like we move our limbs when we want to."

"With that, I want to introduce my good friend, Tyler Davis, who will tell you more about the project."

David passed the microphone to Tyler who was now waiting just below the podium. He reached into his pocket for his cue cards and took the stage. His green eyes looked over the crowd, then down to his notes.

"Thank you, professor," Tyler started, "we wanted to find out whether we could control robotics with our mind, and so we set out to perform some tests. We realized we could make simple things like computer input devices and speakers work easily. The robotics part was quite a bit more difficult, but now that we know how this technology works, we have several plans."

"First, for people who find themselves in Mark's position: unable to speak, our speaker implants work perfectly, right Mark?"

"Right!" Mark chimed in on queue.

"We also know how fast this technology makes us at using computers, so while our initial intention was to just use this to restore some lost function to our lives, we can also market this product to anyone who wants to use a computer more efficiently. That will improve job performance and make people more profitable in their personal and business life."

"But even beyond that, those who are paralyzed, like Mark, finally have a hope of a more independent life. I want to turn it over to Mark to talk about his hopes in the coming months with his project."

"Thank you, Mr. Davis," Mark paused, looking over the crowd. His notes were placed on the podium to read, but his heart told him what to say.

"Every parent wants the best for their kids." He looked to his own parents watching him from the front row. "And they teach their kids how to do the basic skills in life. I found myself, however, in high school, having lost all of those basic skills they had taught me. Since November, I have been unable to get out of bed or to dress myself in the morning. I lost the ability to eat for myself and do many of the skills you all do every day without thinking about it."

He paused, freezing the crowd into dead silence as they hung on every word.

"Two days ago, we finally got this robotic limb to work while attached to my lab bench." He raised the arm in the air for a moment and then put it down. "That day, we attached it to my wheelchair and since that point in time, I have been able to feed myself for the first time since last

November. The old skills my parents taught me are now slowly coming back. And that is our future for this project in my lab. I will not stop until this technology is used to restore all my basic functions. And once we do that, we will hopefully be able to restore a normal life to other people who are also in my situation. Thank you."

The room exploded with applause and a standing ovation. Mr. Jones retook the microphone at the podium.

"We are happy to take a few questions and Mark has agreed to answer some direct questions as well, but please do not crowd him."

The Q&A went on for about thirty minutes with various medical questions, robotics, costs, and a few odds and ends for Mark. They finished that section and worked the room a little more. Mr. Jones received many contacts for people interested in future conversations while Mark grabbed many random objects at the request of curious patrons.

"Mark!" A familiar voice called out.

"Sam! What are you doing here?"

"My company received an invitation. Since I'm the local robotics manager, they sent me to see what this company's up to." Sam examined the arm, "Let me inspect this limb of yours."

He looked up and down the machinery. It was crude and functional, but not really durable. He pointed out several areas of weakness in the device and suggested a few fixes.

"If I can get you the plans, can you make a better version?"

"Of course," Sam offered.

Sam knew where to get the parts they would need and how to make the robot more durable for real-world applications rather than the experimental lab tests of the current device. He also had access to the tools to make it work properly.

"Well, I need to talk to Mr. Jones as well. My boss will not be happy if I don't make a few connections."

Mark wheeled off from his brother-in-law and was greeted by Micheal in an instant.

"Vanilla?" Was his only word.

"What?" Asked Mark.

"Vanilla shake? You said that was your favorite. You always told me that you hate vanilla," Micheal said.

"I do. Not sure what came over me. Maybe it was just nervousness from the crowd."

"Maybe. Still, curious you would go for that, though. It caught us all off our guard."

"Well, I wouldn't worry about it. It was just my nerves. I am sure of it."

Ж

"Were you at the event today?" The slightly overweight manager asked his young programmer.

"Yes, sir. Did you like my 'suggestion'?"

The larger man scowled at the playful language of his subordinate, "What was your suggestion? I was looking for something but I didn't see it."

"Sir, if I remember your instruction, my test was to display something so subtle no one would really see it. That's what I did."

"And just what did you do?" His scowl faded to curiosity while he loosened his tie.

The young man rustled through papers on the desk finally picking up a packet and studying it for a moment, "Aha, here it is."

He handed the stack of papers to his boss who snatched it up and studied it. The young programmer continued, "My study of the logs indicated that the lab team often goes out for milkshakes. The subject always orders chocolate, so I made him order vanilla in front of the crowd. Very subtle, but definitely a change in behavior that we sent through the device. I have been testing this with other behaviors as well over the course of the last couple weeks."

"Interesting. It looks like you did accomplish your goal. I remember him ordering the vanilla shake, but I didn't know to look for that," the man finally looked up from the report with a hint of a smile, "What were the other suggestions you have tested?"

"Well, if you look at page five, we changed the style of music he likes. It actually resulted in him spending less time listening to music. I don't think we have the power to change his opinions; we only have influence over the actual decision-making process."

"Very good. Any issues to report?" Said the manager.

"Not yet, sir. But I have a lot of logs to sift through from the last few days. Perhaps we can get Joe to help?"

"Absolutely not! You know the deal, this part is ultra secure, we can't have anyone else looking into it. Understand?"

"Yes, sir," the young man recoiled.

"Good. I need to be heading off now, do let me know if any issues arise in the logs."

21

In the weeks following the Synaptergy event, the team focused on creating the miniscale robot assistant for full range testing. While the movements were functioning correctly, getting the body stabilized presented a challenge, so they decided on tread-like wheels for the assistant. After a few weeks and some late night research, they finally completed a miniscale prototype robot that Mark could control with the implant. The small scale robot resembled a toy, but it seemed to have a life of its own. Mark moved it across the lab bench, picking up small objects, and carrying out menial task as the testing protocols.

The completion of the smaller robot allowed the up-scaling needed to build the larger scale prototype that Mark could carry on the wheelchair for deployed use. They decided on a form factor that would fold down small enough to fit onto a basket that was added to the back of his chair. With some practice, Mark was able to call the robot out with a special command. It would then extend up to the height of a normal person with two arms able to carry out basic tasks. The time to bring the prototype to the first test took the team nearly a month.

"Robbie experimental protocol test one," Micheal said.

The camera was ready and focused on the back of Mark's wheelchair. The command was issued and the robot reached its arms up, grabbing a bar beneath the top basket. It picked itself up to clear the basket and rolled itself out with a mechanical hum. Finally, it expanded its body up to be about five feet in height while emanating several clicks and clanks.

Mark issued the first command for the robot to pick up, show him, and set down various objects from the lab bench. Small tools, parts, and finally a box of gloves were clumsily grasped as if hesitating to know the correct object. Robbie finally reached for the gloves which sat on the shelf above the lab bench. The arm reached out, grabbed the box of gloves, and slowly turned around handing them to Robert, who received the gloves from the robot's hands.

Robert studied the box of gloves as if he was amazed as to the identity of the object.

"Drop the box," Micheal called out.

"Huh?" Robert looked up.

"Drop it...so we can test how Robbie picks things up from the floor."

He laughed at the absurdity of the moment and dropped the box like it suddenly became scalding to the touch.

Once the box was on the ground and the camera fixated on it, the robot reached down, picking up the box, it handed it back to Robert.

The first test was a success.

"Robbie experimental protocol test two," said Micheal.

The robot rolled over to the printer and pulled the tray out of the bottom, setting it on top of the printer. Then it clumsily reached under the cart, fetching a new paper ream with the stiffness of a man donning a sore back. It opened up the package and inserted the paper into the tray with stiff motions. By now, the robot started obstructing Mark's view, so he had to re-position himself to see what he was doing. The robot was not able to accomplish tasks in automation, only respond to Mark's commands in real time. Once he was again in position to view the printer, he was able to clumsily insert the paper tray back into the printer and fetch papers that Robert printed out.

Finally, pleased with the results, they decided a celebration was in order. Robbie folded himself up and reinserted himself into the basket on the chair and the lab team went down to the café for milkshakes.

Mark wanted to test his ability to use Robbie without help, so Robert and Micheal sat down at their regular booth while Mark approached the counter.

"Two vanillas and a strawberry, please."

While the barista was busy working on the shakes, Robbie was summoned from his basket. When the young barista turned around, she rolled her eyes at the robot staring her down. She shook her head, being used to the various mechanical experiments this group of students always brought in. The robot grabbed the tray and brought it back to the table. Robbie distributed the shakes. Strawberry for Robert, vanilla for Micheal and Mark.

Micheal looked at Mark puzzled, "What's your excuse this time?"

"What do you mean?"

"Why'd you order vanilla again? You're not under stress from a conference this time," said Micheal.

"I am not sure. I still do not really like it, I just keep ordering vanilla. I am not sure why!"

"Does the implant change your taste buds?" Robert interjected.

Mark took a sip of the drink, "Apparently not. I do not really like this. It is OK, but I think I would rather have chocolate!"

"Is there anything else you find yourself doing differently?" Micheal asked.

"Not that I can think of...I did not even notice I ordered this flavor until you said something." Mark sipped again, each mouthful tasting worse to him than the prior gulps; he was now conscious of the despised flavor in his cup. Immediately, he tried thinking back to the last few weeks since the event thinking about everything he did, trying to see if anything else was different. "I have not read anything in a few weeks...well, at least not anything not work related," Mark remembered.

"Is that normal?" Said Micheal.

"No," Mark thought back more. Before last November, he was diligent about reading to rest his mind. During the period he was stuck in his chair it was much the same, except his mom read to him, but once he was able to read again on the computer he had filled the disk with classic novels and new acquisitions alike. He had been as excited as a kid on Christmas with the new collection of books he was eager to read, but since the Synaptergy event, he did not remember reading anything for fun.

"Is it possible you've just been too busy?" Robert asked, reminding them that they have all been really busy with the prototype.

"No. I have watched more television lately, and I do not even like television!"

For the first time since the project began, Mark was feeling a little uneasy. Something lay just off his comfort zone as they continued conjecturing ideas about these changes but did not have any framework to test any theories, so they headed back to the lab.

"Come in!" David answered to the knock on his office door.

The mechanical arm on the wheelchair opened the door enough for Mark to roll in and then shut it behind him.

"I have noticed some strange things lately, professor."

"Like what?"

"Micheal noticed it first," he started, "I keep ordering vanilla milkshakes."

"So?"

"So, I hate vanilla! We were talking about it at the café, and I noticed I have also stopped reading. I always look forward to reading, especially since I have the ability to do it again. My preferences are not changing, just what I decide to do at the moment, like my decision-making is being controlled by something else."

"Hmm..." The professor stood up and turned to look out the window. He studied a group of people on the field outside for a moment. He turned back around to look Mark over again, "What would happen if next time you need to order something, you are interrupted by someone who watches over you, like Micheal? We need to be able to capture the thoughts as they are happening. Think over how we can do that."

"OK," he said, "I will think over anything else that seems different and start making a log of them."

"That would be good. I'll be talking to Tyler soon, so I'll bring this up with him. You'll probably want to talk to the medical team about it, too. Want me to pass on the message or is that something you'll handle?"

"My dad works with John, so I will just let him know, and we will see what can be done about it."

22

"Has Mr. Davis arrived?"

"Right this way, sir." Giordano's had been the new place for David and Tyler to meet to discuss the project. They both loved Italian cuisine, and the company had no issues picking up the bill from the swankiest place in town, particularly after the positive publicity from the press event.

David took the seat across from his old friend and accepted the menu from the maitre d. The wine glasses were already filled with a dry red and the bread basket was missing a roll or two.

"Been here long?"

"A little bit. I had some paperwork to look over and I didn't want to do it at the office, so I popped in early to snack on some rolls."

"Why here instead of the second home?" He asked, referred to Tyler always likening his perfectly arranged office as another home.

"I just needed to get out of there. I wanted to look these papers over somewhere else."

David sensed a little apprehension in his voice.

"You sound just like you did the day before you proposed to Rachael. What's going on?"

"Oh, nothing. Just a lot of responsibilities with this promotion," he said, sliding a small piece of folded paper across the table.

David hid it in his palm and moved his hand under the table. He causally adorned a downward glance that carried the futility of any college student reading text messages in class. The unfolded paper contained a scribbled message, "We need to talk."

David understood the need for caution and discretion, so he did not push any further. Tyler was not a paranoid person, so the note seemed a little off, still, he trusted his long-time friend. In lieu of his original discussion, he focused on the evolution of the project rather than his real purpose for talking to Tyler. The professor was prepared with videos of Project Robbie and by now they were working on schematics for exosuit functionality.

Tyler watched the videos of the robot and the various tasks they had accomplished. Reports were documented and copies of the videos were submitted to the project portfolio. After business, the social discussions began for the remainder of the meal. The final course was completed and the desserts were consumed, another paper slid across the table, which David picked up in the same manner as before. This note ordered, "Meet me at the park on Pineview in an hour."

David knew this park from the drive to Mark's house. It was about twenty minutes from Giordano's, so he doddled a bit in town before driving toward the park. The car halted to a stop in the parking spot next to the park. David did not see any movement, so he instead fixated on the oak trees that were budding and producing tiny leaves. The playground area of the park was lightly coated with last season's brown leaves, though the concrete paths were perfectly clear.

After about five minutes of admiring the quiet landscape, a strange car pulled up to the park and Tyler jumped out of the back seat. He said his thanks and goodbyes, and watched the car drive off before turning to David's silver Honda. He opened the passenger side door taking a seat while pulling some aluminum foil from his jacket.

"Who was that?" Asked David.

"I called a Lyft for a ride. I think I might be followed. Can I have your phone?" Said Tyler.

David relinquished his phone from the inside jacket pocket without hesitation. Tyler quickly wrapped it in the foil.

"Where to?" Asked David, playing the role of a chauffeur.

"Somewhere remote."

David shifted the car into gear and started driving aimlessly, "Tyler, I've never seen you like this before. Is everything OK? Who's following you?"

"I'm not sure anyone is," Tyler said, "I'm just taking precautions. I need to tell you something, but no one can know we're talking."

"Is this about the project?"

Tyler glanced behind him half looking in the back seat but also making sure the car was not being followed.

"Yes. About a month ago, after our first breakthrough when I met you on campus, I had a meeting with Mr.

Jones, the Chairman, and Mr. Meyer. Apparently, Mr. Meyer has a team of people working on the project also, but I don't know to what extent. When I questioned what they were doing, they became cagey about it. I went back through documents and found that they were right: the other team was always in the plan, but while your project was completely detailed, theirs is listed as classified. They're doing something with the medical team, and the scans in the report sort of look identical. I'm not sure if they're real. Oh, and in the meeting, they seemed very interested in the second receiver I delivered...the one that's being used for all the robotics controls."

Tyler stopped to allow David to soak in the information, but he continued after a few seconds, "I pulled the hardware reports and found that the implant may still be receiving data in addition to sending signals to the robotics. There's two-way communication built into it, but the software's encrypted. I pulled the source code, but the files in the system are all corrupted. I have no idea what it's doing but it could be receiving signals in addition to outputting them. I asked Mr. Meyer about this, but he said it was just a function built in for his team."

"Tyler, could these signals impact behavior?" Asked David.

"I don't know. Why?"

"What I wanted to talk to you about is that Mark reported some odd behaviors to me," David said with concern growing in his voice.

He spent the next ten minutes talking about milkshakes and his lack of reading, "All these are very minor, but still very odd behavior for Mark."

"When did this start?" Tyler asked, checking the mirrors again.

"Micheal first noted it during the press event. When Mark went to get a milkshake to show what we could do, he grabbed a vanilla."

"So?"

"So, Mark hates vanilla. Like I said, very minor…easy to miss, even. But still odd when we consider the amount of times we have observed this. He thought it was enough of an oddity to report. Especially since the frequency of these events are increasing," David paused in his explanation long enough for a breath, "Could signals received by the implant be causing this?"

"It's possible, but since we can't see the software drivers, we have no way of knowing."

"Can't you get the code?" Said David.

"Like I said, the code is corrupted. I went to talk to the guys who were debugging it before we started on the project, but they have all been sent to international teams," Tyler paused to rub his neck, "I can't reach any of them."

"What should we do?" David asked, more quietly now.

"I think for now, we watch. We look for anomalies and report them. If someone is doing something nefarious, we don't want to tip our hand that we know anything until we know what we are dealing with," Tyler grew more concerned.

David was thought about the issues before asking, "What about the medical team…not at Synaptergy, but at the hospital. Do they have the real scans? You said the ones you found are all the same."

"I don't know. Is it worth asking about it? I would assume they have everything that is in our reports. There is no way the company would have different internal reports than what the hospital records show," said Tyler.

"Well, let's ask Eric to look at the scans to see if he notices any similarity in them." David thought about this. If Eric notices and raises a flag, it might not be good. "What about Mark. What do we tell him?"

Tyler thought for a few minutes, "Well, let's not tell him we think something is up, but we should make sure he is on the lookout for anything else out of the ordinary."

"Tyler, this project is too significant to stop, and with such vague concerns, I agree we don't want to draw too much attention to things right now. Still, I have some pull with the family, so what if we talk to Eric informally to see if he can get us any other information.”

“Sounds good. I’ll let you handle that, but I’ll take the anomalies to Mr. Meyer to see what he says about it,” said Tyler.

“Deal. Anything else?”

“I think that is about it,” said Tyler, “drop me off a few blocks from home and I’ll walk from there. Go back to the park to take the foil off your phone.”

23

Mark finally found himself useful at home with Robbie’s aid, and even insisted on being assigned chores. The work around the house allowed him to test skills with the robot. He started carrying his own meals from the kitchen to the dinning room and feeding himself. Of course, Robbie carried the food, opened doors and windows, but the mechanical arm on the wheelchair was still receiving the most personal use. He almost enjoyed eating now, particularly since Robbie could make smoothies, but the prototype robot was never waterproofed, so Mark was never able to clean the dishes much to his mom's chagrin.

Even without the ability to wash the dishes, Mark beamed with pride in every new achievement. It was more thrilling to discover his newfound freedom than it was when he first learned how to carry his drink to the table or put a spoon of apple sauce into his mouth by himself. He was starting to see his dreams come true with the help of this new technology.

As for the regular routines, Robbie was able to get him out of bed and into the wheelchair, empowering him to go about most of the day with minimal assistance. He still needed help with cleaning routines of various kinds. Between the robot and the arm, he was able to figure out using the toilet on his own, but showering was out of the question. Also, out of the question was ascending the stairs: his secret and coveted goal. As long as he did not need to approach water or steps, he was now capable of anything he needed to do at home.

Still, the project needed to move ahead, and Mark was as dedicated as ever to working either at the lab or at home. Despite the deep drive and motivation, he also found himself watching more television than ever for reasons he did not fully understand.

"Watching more TV, Mark?" Eric interrupted his thoughts as he sat down at the desk and opened the drawer retrieving the checkbook.

"Yeah...and I do not know why. I do not even like this show, and I have a lot of things I still want to do on the computer tonight."

Eric flipped the television off with the remote and placed it on the entertainment stand as if it were out of reach, and if Mark did not have Robbie with him, it would have been out of reach. "What's the next step in your project?" Eric asked.

"We are trying to move without the wheelchair. The exosuit project is coming along nicely, and I have some maps to pattern for basic things like sitting and standing that will feed through a support structure."

"So you're trying to capture movement groups and map those specifically?" Eric said, tossing the addictive checkbook from his hand and spinning his chair, focusing on his son.

"Yes. We started by looking to isolate each pattern, but that would take a long time to figure out everything. On top of that, the robotics needed to make that work would be overly-complicated. Basically we would need to build a robot with all the muscle groups at once. But this way we can use a prebuilt robotic frame and send the whole group function as a special signal."

"That sounds more efficient than building the whole robot. Does it cause problems if you start with a single message that would be part of the group?"

"Yes, sort of, so we calibrated the software by pausing on a few functions to make sure they were isolated. In reality, it does not cause a lot of issues because you rarely perform the action of starting to sit without committing to sit, so it works out in the long run."

"I never thought of that," Eric said, "but you're right!" He paused for a moment, seeing his paralyzed son as more of a man in that moment. He was not even embarrassed about being out-smarted on basic anatomical chain reactions. "Let's head to the kitchen for a bit!"

Eric filled the water pot for hot chocolate and Mark rolled past him. The mechanical arm on the wheelchair grabbed a glass from the dish strainer, and the chair spun in the direction of the refrigerator. Mark rifled through the top shelf, retrieving the milk. He poured himself a glass and lifted it to his face. Eric watched in puzzlement while small drops of milk spilled out from the partial seal around Mark's mouth. When the cup was placed in the sink, he finally asked,

"Was it good?"

"What? The milk...no?"

"Why did you drink it? You hate milk."

"I know. The same way I hate vanilla milkshakes but I keep ordering them...and the same way I keep watching television, but I do not even like it. It is like something tells me to do things I do not like to do, but I do not realize I am doing it until I catch myself, or rather, someone tells me something I just did! Could the implant be doing this?"

Eric turned white while thinking about the secret photos of the real implant hidden among the tools in the garage. He paused a little longer than he intended to, but was snapped back to present with the loud click and bubbling roar of the electric kettle. "I'm not sure. I'll ask John about it tomorrow."

Mark grabbed the water pitcher while Eric was still stunned in his thoughts. He poured the steaming water into the cups, added the mix, and stirred them.

"Ready?" Mark said, retrieving both cups with one swift motion on the mechanical arm.

"So on to the project," Eric said, following Mark, "What's the plan to get out of the chair? Obviously Robbie can't do that, as impressive as he is."

"We are going to start with braces, like leg and arm braces, but fit them with motors for the functions we need. The braces will act as an exoskeleton for support and the motors will be able to move the joints like our bone joints do."

"When are you working on those?" Eric asked.

"We have the leg braces built and the code is ready to feed inputs. We are planning on testing them tomorrow. The arms are under development, probably set to be finished in the next couple of days. The backbone is the real problem. We need to figure out how to get the thing to stand on its own. I can not keep thinking about straightening my back for stability."

"The brain should do that on its own. Aren't you collecting signals for that?"

"We are," Mark said, "but they are a little more complicated to figure out. Basically, we need to work backwards on that part instead of forwards, pulling gyroscopic data into the mix to send to the program stabilizing the backbone. Once that is done, we are good to go."

They continued talking for about an hour. Mark detailed the various components: the power belt with hot-swapable batteries, a new streamlined speaker for communication, and all the other details that promised to give him the ability to walk on his own. Eric meanwhile gave him some tips for range of motion based on ball joints in the body.

"I can't wait to hear how the leg test goes tomorrow," Eric said, "but for now, we need to head off to bed."

"I will let you know…and talk to John to see if the implant is messing with my brain."

"Will do. Keep letting me know of anything else that happens like that. You said the first time you noticed that was at the press event?"

"Yep," Mark answered on the way to his room.

"Do you need any help?"

"I want to get into bed myself. I will call out when I am done so you know we are good for the night."

24

"Come in, doctor," Mr. Meyer's voice sounded empty, maybe bored.

John walked in, closing the door quietly, save for the faint squeak of the old hinge. Mr. Meyer fixated on a report without looking up at the doctor. He reached to his right, tapping up and down searching with his hands, finally grabbing a scan and handing it to John, still fixing his eyes on the paper, "Here's the scan for the team."

John accepted the roll, opened it up, approached the window to examine the images.

"This is the same scan as last time," His statement shattered the silence, finally causing Mr. Meyer to glance up from the report.

"Yeah. Did you think we actually made a scan during the day of the event? We know this is safe."

"Well, the problem is every scan's slightly different. If anyone on the team examines this closely, they will also notice it's the same. Even the dates match!" Said John.

"What?!" He threw the report to the desk and slammed his rolling chair into the wall while hastily standing up, "I was told they changed enough to not look identical!"

He opened the cabinet to retrieve his copy of the last scan John was given. The rolled up scan was opened up and held up to the window to see the light comparing the date inscribed on the bottom.

"Jessica?"

Within a few seconds, the petite secretary opened the door. "Yes, sir?"

"Can you get me Jason on the line, please?"

"Right away, sir," she said.

The scans were indeed identical, right down to the date.

"Did we just get a second copy?" John asked.

"There're only supposed to be two copies of this: ours and yours."

"Line one, sir," Jessica's voice was muffled through the closed inner office door.

The duplicate scan was discarded to the floor and Mr. Meyer put on a mean demeanor to push the line one button on the desk phone.

"Jason, the scan I have is identical to the last one. What's going on?" Mr. Meyer demanded.

There was a pause while Jason was talking. John only heard a whispered, scratchy voice on the other end of the line. He strained to pick up on some words, but was not able to understand anything.

"OK, get on it quickly, we said the scans were done and the medical team lead from the hospital's here."

The phone slammed down, "Sometimes I don't know about that guy. He'll call back in a few minutes. In the meantime, have a look at this report."

He snatched up the report he was reading earlier and handed it up to the doctor.

John caught the first glimpse of the report: "REPORT OF BEHAVIORAL ANOMALIES submitted by Tyler Davis."

In the report, Tyler detailed the anomalies in behavior providing a list of odd events as relayed by the robotics team.

"We know this thing's safe, John, but what could be causing Patient Zero to change personal preferences so radically?" Asked Mr. Meyer.

"It says here that his preferences have not changed, just specific decisions in predictable situations. Why was this reported? Teenagers are often fickle in their actions," explained John.

"Apparently it raised the concerns of the team, so they included it."

"Well," John said, "if he changed his preference for flavor of the milkshake, that could be explained by brain trauma, but just changing what he orders at restaurants? Not sure. I think we should have another legitimate scan just to be safe."

"I'm not sure, John. That might need to go into the record, and we're trying to keep the freaky look of this out of the reports."

"Hello?" Mr. Meyer shifted his focus to the phone. Jason called back to report on the error. Apparently, the old file was still on the computer and the wrong scan was printed. He was printing the new copy and promised to delete all the evidence of the change as soon as it was confirmed. "Thanks, Jason. Right away, please." He hung up the phone, "The new scan will be right here. In the meantime, what do we do about these anomalies?"

"Since they're reported, we have to get to the bottom of it. It either has to be addressed by the medical team, in which case a lot of independent tests are going to be done, or else the robotics team will need to get to the bottom of it."

"The robotics team will have to do it. They are the only ones who won't do the extra scans. But like you said, 'teens are fickle' in their choices. What if we just write it off as a youth changing his mind? That angle could work. We keep looking at the safety on our end and the possibilities on the robotics team," suggested Mr. Meyer.

"That could work, but I would personally like to know more about this; it's the type of thing that independent verification will want to see more work on."

"Then we get the testimony of a psychiatrist to lay it to rest and leave it at that," Mr. Meyer said.

"Can I do one more off the record scan, Mr. Meyer." John asked, "I need to know for my own conscience what is going on."

A knock at the door interrupted Mr. Meyer's thoughts, "Come in!"

A sour-faced middle-aged man opened the door clutching a new scan. He walked past John to hand the scan to Mr. Meyer.

"Thank you, Jason. Do you know Doctor Jacobs?"

A steady hand reached out, "Nice to finally meet you, doctor."

"Likewise."

Mr. Meyer opened the scan examining the date to see it was different from the prior one. "This looks better to me, how 'bout you?"

John took the scan to the window looking it over. After briefly examining each one, he was happy to see it was a good scan, different from the other ones in the project records, but still containing the data the company wanted to portray.

Jason was stroking his mustache awaiting the final word from the doctor. Once he approved, Jason was dismissed and the door silently latched shut.

"So what about it, Mr. Meyer?"

"About what?" Mr. Meyer asked.

"Another scan? I want to make sure the implant has stopped growing."

"I am confident it has, doctor. As for the scan, I want a few days to think it over."

John let out a sigh of disapproval, but lifted his countenance, "OK, just let me know...I need to report back to the team now." He took his copy of the scan and left Synaptergy headquarters.

ӂ

Mark was up early in the morning about the same time John was talking to Mr. Meyer. He was ready to make it into the lab, having read through his protocols several times, so he knew exactly where to start on the leg brace structure. He went rapidly through his morning routine as far as he could go and worked on the computer until it was time for lunch. Mark was anxious to go into the lab early to get a start, but Micheal had classes in the morning, so there was no point in that.

When he did make it into the lab, he went right to work testing the program that would be placed onto the board. He was confident in the signals, so his two assistants strapped the braces onto his legs while he programmed the board with his implant and made sure the program was properly inserted.

As soon as power started running through the board, the leg braces started twitching a little. Mark had to clear his mind, but once he did, the motion stopped. They built in some safety protocols to make sure they could not move against the joints to minimize the risk of breaking bones if gears ran in the wrong direction.

The first test was commenced. The camera was ready and the explanations were dictated to the camera. Mark used his mind to lift his right leg for the first time since November. This was followed by the left. Up. Down. Up. Down. Finally, he raised it up and then rolled the ankle bone around. It was comfortable and natural, which Mark vocalized for the camera. This experiment was considered a success so the team started working on the programming and hardware for the back structure which, like a spine, provided support for standing up. This was a difficult task, but the plans were already set into motion.

The final measurements were made, code snippets analyzed, and a few board structures were proposed that used gyroscopic sensors attached to an Artificial Intelligence algorithm to maintain balance. Within a few weeks, the team was able to create a back, arms, and a neck structure marking the completion of the basic code for the exosuit. He was fitted for the various components in the second week of June. The team tested a few protocols, and then finally, they were ready for the official test.

David took a seat in the chair to watch the progress his students were making. Robert took the position at the camera today while Mark was seated in a chair being braced by Micheal from behind. The camera started rolling.

"Project Freedom, Test 1"

After a brief hesitation, Mark stood up. It was as natural to him as any other time in his teenage life. His thought process was no more or less complicated than it was before he learned to walk. He arose, stood on his right leg, then his left. He took a few steps forward and then a few steps back; he rotated his back, raised his arms, turned his head. Mark was able to perform perfectly with the aid of the exosuit.

David gave him a list of commands from tying shoes to handing him objects. He moved the printer, filled it with paper, retrieved printouts, and a variety of other basic human undertakings. It was freeing, more than an experiment; it was restoration of his life.

"Bring the camera along. We are going to the café!"

Mark led the way out of the lab and the team followed him passed the elevator, and to the steps.

"Careful, Mark," David called out, keeping a cool head that this was still an experiment.

"Get ahead of me, please," Mark directed toward Micheal, realizing David was correct about the possible dangers of walking down steps again.

He took the stairs slowly at first to make sure he would not stumble, but then he realized they were just as natural as before. Still, he grasped the rail until he reached the landing. The camera was still rolling when he headed out the door.

Now in the café, the regular attendant looked Mark up and down. "Wow. Did you guys really get that kid out of the wheelchair in a robotics lab?" She was addressing everyone in the group.

"Yep," Mark replied, still not able to smile much, but the speaker, which Robert was now carrying, spoke for him.

Mark turned back to the lab assistant holding the speaker and made a glib remark about holding his head in his hand.

"We need to get a more condensed speaker from Tyler," he said more seriously after the laughter was over.

Mark started to order the shakes with Micheal by his side. When he called out, "One strawberry and two vanilla," Micheal immediately interrupted, "Make mine a chocolate today, please."

Mark and Micheal caught each other's glances, "I did it again, huh?"

"Yes, you did. What was your thought process?"

The barista stood confused, "So what am I making?"

"One of each flavor," Mark answered, before turning back to Micheal, "I knew I was ordering for everyone and remembered your orders, but I lost track of what I wanted for myself, and just ordered the number we needed."

Micheal clarified, "Like you are losing conscientiousness in the ordering process?"

"Yes, that is a good way to describe it. Sort of absent-minded...like a kid."

The order was ready in a moment, so they each grabbed their shakes and headed to their regular booth. They laughed over the successes and failures of the last few months. Mark was glowing with happiness over finally being able to walk on his own, though he was not able to make the facial expressions to demonstrate it. It was a monumental day in the lab, one they were all looking forward to seeing. They discussed their next steps, followed by determining when they would go to Synaptergy to show the progress.

They returned to the lab to check the logs built into the exosuit, ran a few tests, and checked on the status of the batteries. The team still needed to work on the belt to hold the extended power supply and the section to hold the new condensed speaker. The suit was not ready for Mark to wear home yet, but he was working in anticipation to finalize everything.

After the diagnostics, they helped Mark back into the prison of his wheelchair to get ready to go home.

25

Eric opened his locker at the hospital to prep for the day causing a small piece of paper to flutter down through the air, landing on his shoe. He picked up the curious note and looked around for a hint of who might have left it. He opened the paper and read the scribbling.

"Meet me at the park at 8:00. Destroy this note."

The note induced a sudden uneasy feeling in the pit of his stomach. It was unsigned, but he thought it resembled, though hastily written, John's scribbling. He tried to put concern out of his mind. Eric carried the note to the hand washing sink and scrubbed and tore it into pieces while he scrubbed his hands and arms for the start of his shift. The note was perfectly macerated into pulp that sloshed down the drain with soapy water.

The day was long, and he knew the night would be just as long. He finally made his way through the uneasy shift, often drifting ahead to 8:00, 8:00, 8:00 in his mind. He put it out of his thoughts and left for home to talk with the family, but he kept the secret meeting from them. They had their usual walk to the park and an unusually quiet dinner. Finally, he spoke up while sliding his fork under a pile of peas.

"I have a social engagement tonight at 8:00. Something to do with the hospital staff."

"Isn't that pretty late?" Asked Susan.

"Yes, but these after hours events often are," he lied, "I will call when I get there to let you know when to expect me."

"Still," she paused, "why didn't you mention this until now?"

"I'm not excited about it. I'm tired and would rather not go out again tonight." He was not exactly excited, but certainly intrigued by the note and secret meeting. He kept reserved and continued in a softer tone, "I guess it just slipped by mind."

"Eric!" She yelled, then pausing once she caught Mark's eye, she softened her tone, "we'll talk about it later," she completed, mirroring his action on the peas that Eric ultimately ignored.

Voices were heard upstairs shortly after dinner that started loud but faded off into silence, which meant whispers. Mark did not know what was going on, but after the closed-door meeting, Susan seemed more at peace with Eric leaving.

He left a little before eight and drove off toward the park, reaching the curbside parking spot in a minute, but waiting in the car another ten minutes: the length of his regular commute. The sun was slowly sinking into the horizon but the park was still light with the glow of dusk in spring. He waited. Finally, another car pulled up into the spot just in front of him. The white Ford Taurus had lightly tinted windows, which hid the driver in the edge of evening. Eric looked at the back of the car admiring the 'Eagle Scout' bumper sticker, then the driver-side door was kicked open from the inside and John stepped out of the car.

"Hi John!" He yelled out, but John put his forefinger up to his lips to silence him.

Once he was nearby he finally spoke in more hushed tones, "This project is getting weird, Eric. I've worked on some hush-hush medical teams, but this is getting…" he stopped to look for the proper words, but Eric cut in, "Weird?"

They caught each other's eyes with a smirk. Eric continued, "Does this have to do with the anomalies in Mark's preferences?"

"Partially. The thing is, the scans are weird as you know, but the company is exerting a lot of effort to hide the real images. The followup scan was not a scan from the day of the Synaptergy press release; they said they never did one. When I went to the office, they tried to give me another copy of the first scan, but they finally gave me a totally fake image. Mr. Meyer is behind the fake scans, but he is just as puzzled by the anomalies as we are."

"So what do we do?" Eric asked.

"I want to order another scan, but Mr. Meyer will not allow it. I almost want to do one without telling them, but the whole imaging team is working with Synaptergy, so I'm not sure I could pull it off without word getting back to Mr. Meyer. But once we received the last scan, and he rejected the ordering of the new one, I think I've been followed. I can't be sure, but I have seen the same truck follow me home and to work, on the block late at night, and even on the edge of the ER parking lot when I arrive for my shifts. That's why I drove the wife's car today. I'm still watching out."

"Did you ask Mr. Meyer about it?" John said, "about being followed?"

"I haven't seen him in two weeks, since the last scan I picked up for the hospital team, not that I would ask him about that kind o' thing anyway. If he is involved in something, he is the last person I want to know that I suspect something. You need to keep that picture of the scan a secret. I think that will be the key if something goes down."

"Goes down?" Eric laughed, "Are you expecting a gang bang?"

"Well, anything can happen in a case like this," John said, "we need to be extra careful."

"What about the research team? Do they know anything is off?"

"Just the anomalies. They are the ones that filed the report about them. I think someone knows what's up, but if it's Mr. Meyer, he needs an Oscar for his performance."

"I think I have a friend who runs the scans in the next city over. I can ask about doing a scan off the record if that would help," Eric offered.

"Yes, let's plan on that. Keep me informed, but we need to keep our contact on this subject pretty quiet. The last time I was involved in a project when I got these intuitions, my partner ended up dead for asking the wrong questions."

Eric paused to take in the seriousness of the situation, "OK...how do we proceed?"

John's old training was starting to kick back in, "First, keep information that we learn documented, but we need to be careful about it. Discreetly keep notes on paper, but in code. Avoid computer files or anything on a network.

And we only talk about it here, or if we find another park…anything that is likely to have very few people and wide open spaces. We need to find a good code to communicate our need to talk."

"What about the expiration dots?"

"Expiration dots?" John asked.

"Yes, at the hospital. We have the colored dots for expiring medications and supplies. Use the purple for 8:00, green for 5:00. Put the dot on the bottom of the locker as a signal to meet up," said Eric.

"Perfect. That will work just fine. Get a small notebook you can keep hidden and write in code the things we know. If I learn anything else, we'll meet up."

They just finished their second lap around the park and arrived at the two cars parked on the side of the street. Eric got into his car and started up the engine.

John started his wife's car and U-turned on the street to go back toward his house. He left the residential block and jumped on the highway to bypass town. Traffic flowed on the two lane road hovering just above the speed limit. John turned on the radio and flipped through the buttons to find his station when a blinding light flashed in his mirrors. The car behind him rode higher than his Taurus.

"Probably a semi," he said aloud to himself.

But the car got closer and closer. The brush guard on the vehicle caught his eye and his thoughts went back to the white truck he thought was following him.

"Did that truck have a brush guard?" He yelled to his memory.

His memory responded in a flash recalling that it did. The truck he had seen following him around town could be the one behind him now! He lightly tapped the brake to kick off the cruise control allowing his car to slow down below 50 mph. The truck riding his tail didn't slow, but inched closer, now nearly blinding him. The corner of his eye caught another vehicle passing with high beams blinding him in his side mirror. This new truck beside him paced his speed and slowly slid into his lane inching closer to his left while the truck behind him closed the gap.

John slammed the gas to speed away, but the little Taurus was not a match for the eight-cylinder diesel engines tailing him. The trucks reset again inching him to the shoulder, but now at an accelerated rate. He grabbed the wheel firmly with his white knuckles gripping tightly to keep the car as straight as possible straddling the road and the shoulder. An overpass guide rail was in his path. He only had two options: push back against a truck that was inching closer into his lane, or hit the rail. He pushed against the truck to move from the lane, but it was a futile attempt, the truck pushed back kicking the Taurus onto the ramp of railing. The car straddled on the rail for a moment before flying down into the busy road below, directly into the middle of two-way traffic. The loud crash was heard for a mile while the two trucks sped off down the road.

26

"I'm home!" Eric yelled out to a house quiet, except for a news report blaring louder than usual from the television.

"Look at this, Dad!"

Susan and Mark crowded the television with news coverage of an accident. The camera was panning over the carnage while the reporter was narrating how a car dropped into oncoming traffic from an overpass.

Eric looked at the scene of wreckage fixing on the mass of white, twisted metal with a torn Eagle Scout sticker on the back bumper.

"That looks like John's car! I just saw him driving it a few minutes ago!"

The impact was just setting in, but his phone jogged his emotions further, ringing the tone assigned to a call from the hospital ER. He took it from his pocket, studying the contact he already knew was displayed.

"It's the hospital…" Eric started coldly. "Hello? Yes…I am watching the report…right away, sir."

They both looked at Eric, waiting for him to say something. He paused for a moment, still staring at the phone.

"I need to go. They need all hands at the hospital." He slipped the phone back into his pocket and started back to the garage door, sighing loudly like a low hiss.

"Eric!" Susan called after him, leaping off the couch. She caught him in the kitchen and whispered, "Maybe it isn't John."

He agreed with her in words but denied it in his heart, remembering the conversations they just had, knowing it was his car, and wondering if this really was an 'accident'.

"I'll call you when I can. Don't wait up for me." He kissed his wife goodbye and opened the door, rushing back to the hospital cautiously, but quickly.

Eric pulled into the doctor's lot, scanning the area for any of John's cars to no avail. He rushed into the staff entrance of the hospital toward the ER department. The evening events were too garbled in his mind, so his medical autopilot guided his actions. He did not remember washing and prepping before landing on the floor to receive orders. Patients were still being wheeled in from the ambulance port, so he went for the first person on the waiting list and begun the various tests and procedures.

Patient after patient was triaged and stabilized. Finally, the staff was able to take a break and share group concerns.

"Where's John?" Eric finally asked the attending doctors.

"Not sure. He didn't pick up his phone when I called."

"Did you try his house?"

"Yes, we tried all the numbers we have."

After a moment of pause, Eric finally broke the somber silence in the room again. "I just talked to John not long before the accident. He was driving his wife's car, and the footage of the accident matches the description of the car down to the bumper sticker. We need to find out."

Eric left the rest of the staff to retrieve his phone from the locker room. First was John's cell phone, but no answer, then his house phone and the same. Finally, he called his wife's phone.

"Eric?" A teary voice hesitantly answered.

"Yes. Is John with you?" Eric said.

"John died," she sobbed in tears. After a sniffle and some regained composure, "He said he was going to talk to you. What happened?"

"I am so sorry," He paused, "we met up at the park to talk for a while, then we both went our ways. The last time I saw him, he was driving home."

"Why were you talking so late?" She demanded.

"It was just an evening to walk and talk," he lied, wanting to tell her about the conversation, but not over the phone, nor in the hospital locker room. "I can have Susan go over there to help you if you need."

"Please," she sniffled again.

"I'll call her now. Again, I am so sorry, and please let me know of anything else we can do."

Eric hung up the phone, cried to himself for a few minutes before dialing home.

Ж

"Hello?" Susan was hesitant to pick up the phone when Eric called.

"John was in the accident," he sobbed.

Susan waited a moment. "What can I do?"

"Right now, I need you to take Mark and go to Debbie's house. I'll be here all night, so I'll go over there in the morning." He stopped long enough to build more courage, "I don't want to alarm you, but there are suspicious circumstances." He hesitantly told her just enough to make her more aware of her surroundings, but without revealing the issues in his heart.

"I love you," she finally said, being partially cut off by a dead line.

"Mark. We need to go!" She called out, forgetting that Mark was on the back patio looking at the stars.

"Is it so? What will we do on the project now?" Mark was talking aloud to Orion in the sky, "why did it have to be an accident? I hate accidents…"

A tear rolled down his cheek, but he brushed it away with the mechanical arm attached to the wheelchair. The silence of the evening was broken by the electric whirring of the gears and on the arm, and the cold steel focused his attention to the now-cold teardrop while he was brought back to November 19th in his mind. The bus drove off leaving him behind and it was getting too cold to walk to the college, but he would be late even if he did. He thought about his options and looked around. Jeremy was just now coming out of the school doors heading to the student parking lot.

"Hey, Jeremy!"

He turned around and scowled at Mark before busting a slight smile, "What's up, dork?"

This was not the tone of a friend, but more in the way a bully would say it when he outgrew schoolyard antics.

"Are you heading to town? I missed the bus and need a ride to the college."

"I'm not going there."

"Are you going closer to the college than here?"

"Yeah…I'll give you a lift," Jeremy said, "we need to wait for Mike, though."

Mike was an old friend of Mark's, but they went their ways when Mark became more interested in his academic passions while Mike focused on the temporal pleasures of life.

"'Sup, Mark."

"Mike. How are you?"

"Fine, now that this crappy day is done. You comin' to hang with us today?"

"Nah, he needs to get to the college, so I figured we'd take 'em."

The three boys got into the car and Jeremy started the souped up engine, squealing his tires out of the school parking lot while driving erratically, bouncing from line to line on the road, barely staying inside his lane. It reminded Mark of the time his dad let him steer from his lap, but the car looked to passers' by like a drunken bank robber fleeing the scene.

The two boys in the front seat kept laughing at Mark while his white knuckles grasped the backseat handle like a little terrified kid on his first roller coaster ride.

"Maybe you should slow down a bit?" Mark finally called out from the back seat.

His protests were the fuel for the next testosterone-induced antics.

"Nah. I'm driving too slow, actually," Jeremy yelled back, hitting the accelerator harder, revving the engine up another gear. Mark gripped the handle tighter, pulling himself to the door.

Jeremy slowed down just enough to turn down a back road. "This is a shortcut to the college!" He yelled out while Mike cranked up the radio to the old 'Gangta's Paradise' song.

Once post-turn, the car accelerated faster down the road. Jeremy and Mike looked back at Mark, laughing about the terror in his eyes, not seeing the true reason for the momentary dilatation in his pupils. Jeremy fixed back onto the road seconds too late to see the road twisting around a bend and being replaced by a tree in the path of the speeding car.

Brakes squealed and the wheel cut to the left providing just the conditions necessary to begin a death roll. The G-force was felt by all three boys, but only for a split-second. The terror in their eyes ended when the side door of the car smashed full speed into the tree, and Mark's world went dark.

"Mark!"

He flinched out of his memories and loudly gulped a breath of air.

"What?!"

"Were you sleeping?" Susan asked.

"No, just thinking."

"We need to go," she said now calmly.

"Where to?" Mark inquired.

"There's no time. Just gather everything you need for the night."

Mark went quickly to an emergency checklist he made, so he would not forget any charging cables or other important things needed for his new robotic life. He checked the weather to see what clothes he might need and clumsily packed a bag with the mechanical arms on the side of the wheelchair.

"Do you have everything?" Susan asked, flinging a bag over her shoulder.

"I think so. Where are we going?"

He followed her out to the van and took his spot in the back. The garage door opened and the van pulled out and headed toward John's house.

Susan said, "John passed away tonight, Mark."

"In the accident?"

"Yes…and your dad said there are suspicions around it all, but he did not say what they were. We need to go to be with his wife for the night."

The next few minutes were uncomfortably silent until finally Mark pierced the quiet again, "Was it related to the project?"

"I don't know. Why would it be?"

"We have noticed some weird things. I keep wanting to listen to horrible music and order things I hate. It almost feels like someone is controlling what I do. We reported it to the project last week."

"Why didn't I know about this?" Demanded Susan.

"I just never thought it was important enough to tell you. Dad knew. I think he talked to John about it, but David filed the reports with Tyler."

They were again silent. Too silent; processing the implications of what would occur if someone was actually tinkering with his desires, particularly since they were creating robotic parts being controlled with his mind.

"I am calling David." He finally broke the silence again.

The phone under his mind's control dialed the number at his command.

"Hello?"

"Hi Professor. It is Mark."

"Mark. You're up late. What's going on?"

"Did you file the anomaly report?" Mark asked.

"Yes, I sent it to Tyler the day we talked last week. Why?"

"John died tonight, and dad is not saying much, but he thinks it is suspicious. He went to talk to John tonight, but John never made it home. We are wondering if it has anything to do with the project."

"Tyler would not…" He never finished the sentence. Immediately David went back to his odd conversation in the park. It was like he was putting things together in real time, changing the direction of his words.

"…not what?" Mark finally interrupted his thoughts.

"Nothing. Where are you now?"

"We are going to John's house. Dad told us to go over there for the night," said Mark.

"OK. I'll see if I can reach Tyler and call you back. Will you be up for a while?"

"Yes. Call back any time."

The phone hung up, and instantly Mark and Susan had a sense of concern.

"Why did he hesitate, Mark?"

"I am not sure. He trusts Tyler, and I would think he would let me in on any concerns he had."

Again, the awkward silence filled the van looking for a place to tinker with their private thoughts and concerns.

Before silence was broken again, they pulled up into the driveway. The van parked abruptly and the e-brake was applied creating the rough clicking sound that echoed in the four corners of the van.

"We're here," Susan finally announced as though the destination needed to be confirmed. Perhaps it was just to change the topic or clear the emptiness hovering in the air. They opened the doors and were met by Debbie who collapsed into Susan's arms, sobbing. It was a long embrace, which would have been uncomfortable without the present circumstances. Once it was over, Debbie refocused becoming a host, seeing that everyone had things they needed for the night.

Once everyone was settled in, the ladies went to the dining room table to mourn and Mark laid on the couch thinking of the progress but also having new fears about the perceived weirdness. His phone suddenly jarred him from his reflections.

"Mark. When will you be to the lab tomorrow?" David said on the other end of the phone.

"I do not know."

"Can you get there early? I can pick you up if need-be. I just talked to Tyler, and he wants to meet as soon as we can in the morning."

"Yes. I will call in the morning if I need a ride, otherwise I will be there early."

The call was over as abruptly as it began, and then Mark slipped quietly to sleep on the couch.

27

Mark arrived at the lab just after 8:00 the following morning, and Tyler was already talking to the professor when Mark knocked at the office door. David opened the door with his forefinger pressed against his lips to request silence. Mark darted his gaze between the two men, trying process if this were a joke of some kind, but he complied in silence, and nodded his head to the best of his ability. Tyler then stood up and took the speaker out of the wheelchair basket, turned it off, and then placed it into a foil-wrapped box.

"Sorry, Mark," Tyler said, "I know you will not be able to respond, but I wanted to tell you a few things without the speaker being nearby, as a precaution."

Tyler unfolded his mounting concerns about the project. "It started before your lab was involved when we noticed that the implant was able to receive signals. The coding guys said they patched everything up, but once the application was compiled, all the developers were let go and their forwarding addresses have been erased. I think I noticed the implant still being able to receive signals, but I can't confirm it."

He paused his explanation long enough for Mark to absorb the information. He nodded in understanding, so Tyler continued.

"There's also another team at Synaptergy that's working on the project without our involvement. They are a medical team, but the whole project is classified, so I can't see what they are doing. John was the liaison physician on the project, but there's a medical team at the company that's also leading the way, but my bosses do not want me knowing anything about it."

Again, he paused, "But I think there's still two-way communication that's connected by the new receiver that we are using for the robotics. It is possible that someone is either recording what signals are being input or even sending signals out. We are discussing if this is related to your weird anomalies.”

When they were done talking, he opened up the box to retrieve the speaker. It was powered on returning Mark's voice.

“There is an ACAT in the lab. Get it.” Mark requested.

David retrieved the device and set it up for Mark to use. Tyler returned the speaker to the box. Mark realized again how helpless he was without the implant, but questions needed answering. He fumbled with the old ACAT, piecing together words in barely comprehensible sentences. He spoke with slow, robotic tones.

“CAN...WE...SEE...SOFTWARE...FOR...DEVICE?”

“No, it's compiled, proprietary, and the source code is not in the project files,” Tyler answered.

“CAN...WE...MONITOR...OUTPUT?”

“Probably,” David chimed in, “the board uses a SIM to access the network, so we can route all the traffic through a VPN connected to Wireshark on the endpoint computer.”

“That might raise a flag if someone sees all the transmissions coming from a lab computer while the system has a cellular connection.”

"INSTALL...WIRESHARK...BOARD...COLLECT... LOGS...LOCALLY," Mark pieced together just enough for the computer experts to understand his idea.

"That would work," Tyler agreed, "It will only collect a sample of daily data, but this approach will mask our research on any network we control."

"WHAT...ABOUT...SPEAKER?"

"Yes, this speaker could also be sending data back to the company."

"VPN...MOST...USED...CONNECTIONS."

"Yes, install a VPN here, and at Mark's house to track the data being sent back in those locations, so we can at least collect most of what the speaker might be doing," David said.

"OK...SPEAKER...PLEASE."

David went to work setting a program to log all the data from the implant, and the three determined it best not to let the rest of the team in on the application or the data being collected.

The three of them finished installing the applications and connections they needed before Robert and Micheal returned from classes, and Mark was ready to move on with the next phase of the exosuit project. Tyler had brought with him the final pieces for the belt structure including the new speaker, so the team went to work fixing the belt, attaching the new extended batteries and the new speaker. Other than being waterproofed, the suit was completed and ready for extended testing.

The research team prepped the camera for another test of the suit. Tyler was able to watch first hand as Mark stood up and performed some basic tasks. The official in-lab tests were complete, so Mark was able to do some basic life testing. They again visited the vending machine where Mark was able to select the Skittles, retrieve them from the machine, and open them up. He also opened doors, navigated stairs, and generally was able to live his life as he did before the accident, though with more crude mannerisms.

The whole team and Tyler walked to the café where Mark ordered the shakes and was able to bring them to the table. He only became conscious of his order, when he sipped the cup to find strawberry flavor. Not his favorite but better to him than vanilla. It was still an anomaly, but they were not concerned considering the present success.

After the discussions in the café, Tyler went back to his office while the rest of the team returned to the lab for some more diagnostics. Mark slipped the new VPN log into the files to examine at home apart from the lab. He was sitting in a chair at the desk glancing over reports when Eric walked in.

"Mark? Nice suit!"

Mark stood up and turned to his dad. "What do you think?" He raised his arms up and spun around just like he saw his mom style new dresses every time she brought a new one home.

"Incredible!" Eric walked toward his son looking up and down, admiring the gears, support, and wire railings. "Is it hard to control?"

"No," Mark answered, "It is built to be as natural as moving real limbs. Simple and seamless."

"Do you need to take it off to go home?" Eric said.

"No. We are taking it home tonight. We need to get the wheelchair down to the van, though. Do you want to ride in it today?"

"Why not?" Eric took a seat in the wheelchair and started controlling it more clumsily than Mark had. Practice makes perfect as they say, but Eric was far from practiced at steering a wheelchair.

Mark pushed the button for the elevator and entered quickly. Eric made the attempt at entry, but hit the edge of the door on the way in, "This is harder to control than you make it look!"

"I know, right. Not the place I wanted to be since the accident."

Eric was silent. His emotions overcame him in realizing how limited his son's movements have really been. While he could stand up at any time and get out, Mark was not afforded such luxury.

The elevator door opened as a causal joke ended the silence. They headed to the side parking lot where the van was parked in the nearest spot.

"Hop out, Dad. I will move the chair into place."

Eric stood up out of the chair with the simplicity his son always wished he could. Mark took the seat and causally steered the chair into the locked position in the van before jumping out of it himself. He closed the sliding door and opened the passenger side door and got into the seat next to Eric.

"Where is Mom?" Mark finally asked.

"Still with Debbie. We'll go get her later, but I need to head to the house first."

"Are you just getting home from the hospital?"

"Yes. We had a lot of wounded people in the accident. We just finalized diagnosis of the last patient. Three people are still there, but there's nothing else to do for now."

The two were as silent as a father and son often are while riding together. Finally, Mark asked, "How did the accident happen?"

"The authorities are not sure. We know it was John's car that flew off the overpass into traffic below, but no one really knows why it happened."

"I heard Debbie say the police have a lot of questions. Is that true?"

"Well, Mark, there're some more things going on here, but I don't know if that has anything to do with it."

There was more silence, and Eric was growing uncomfortable in his lies.

"Is the project at the center of it?" Mark asked.

Eric cleared his throat, unsure of what to say and what not to say. He wanted to spill all about the conversation with John and the scan hidden in the garage. He wanted to tell his son that the implant could never be removed. Eric was short on words and at his emotional wits end. Just when he was not sure if the silence could endure, he took the turn onto Sycamore and found his words, "Home at last."

"Dad? Is the project at the center of it?" Mark asked again.

"Let's talk about it later, Mark."

There was no mistaking in Mark's mind that the implant in his head was at the center of the controversy. This made his imagination run wild knowing about the conversation he had with David and Tyler. He was now more anxious than ever to examine the logs from the VPN traffic, but he worried there would not be time.

"Fine, Dad. How long are we going to be home?"

"Just long enough for me to shower and grab some things, and then we need to head out to Debbie's house to see mom. We can talk when we get there."

The van settled into the parking spot. They both looked back at the empty wheelchair and looked at each other.

"Let's just leave it in here." They were in agreement.

28

Eric strolled up the ramp into the kitchen with the same stride of anyone who was awake for thirty-six hours. Mark, however, entered more causally, being absorbed in the moment of walking into the house. He walked up the ramp, stooping to see the old steps underneath. He straightened up and stepped into his kitchen closing the door behind him.

Mark knew his dad's routine, and that he would probably have about fifteen minutes. Thinking through his priorities, he wanted to bring the ACAT with him if they were going to talk about the project, so he grabbed the old device and set it in the van before returning to the bottom of the steps.

He stared at the steps for a moment. For so long, he passed by those stairs in the wheelchair longing to go up, but never wanting any help up to the upper level of the house. Mark relished the moment he could walk up those stairs he ascended thousands of times in his life. It was his secret goal; one he never told anyone. After a few deep breaths, he took a step up, and then another. One after another for the first time up the steps in seven months, he beamed with joy as he took slow paces down the hallway.

His chest pounded in anticipation as he stepped closer and closer to his old childhood bedroom. He cherished each moment and breathed in deeply, reaching for the doorknob. Another breath later and the knob crackled clockwise and the hinges creaked as the door swung open. Memories rushed into his mind in an instant. He thought about the last time he left that bedroom on November 19th.

"Mark! You will be late! Come on!" His mom yelled up the steps, stirring something in a bowl that was likely pancake batter.

He stood in front of the mirror brushing a comb through his hair, trying to conceal the fact that he just woke up. He looked up and down his scrawny body studying his appearance. Mark had never changed his shirt from the night before, so he pulled it up over his head messing up the prior comb job. He gave the shirt a toss landing it perfectly in the gap between the bed and the wall, "Too bad I can't do that in gym class!" He said to himself while rummaging through the dresser for something to wear. He slid his favorite beige sweater over his head and ran the comb through his hair one more time before running out the door.

Mark looked down the hallway as if watching his past self running out the door while he stood there. His eyes glanced to the bed and moved down to see the shirt he tossed was still there. He looked around the room, and apart from some dust, nothing was different. It was a perfectly preserved time capsule of the time when he was a normal high school senior.

He stood in the doorway looking straight ahead to his bed with the nightstand obscured, but just beyond it. To the left was his desk and dresser. He was brought back immediately to his experimenting with robotics toys, classes and studying, and all the other things he used to do in the privacy of his bedroom while he grew from a little boy into a student of robotics.

Mark walked into the center of the bedroom and sat down in the middle of the floor thinking, transporting himself in his mind to his childhood. At once, he was a child playing with his new Tetrix kit, building crude robotics that fascinated his imagination. Somewhere in that awkward transition between childhood and adolescence when boys sometimes want to play with their toys but other times are embarrassed by them, this kit gave him the best of both worlds. He had the ability to build something like the Bionicals of his childhood, but there was a grown up elegance to robots that could be controlled with a computer.

In his memories, he was working on an arm attached to a block that, when set next to something with just the right size and shape, the metal, two-pronged claw could grab it most of the time. He glanced to his dresser to see the old arm still sitting there like a skeletal model; a dead artifact to his earliest robotic creations.

"Dinner time!" He remembered, so he grabbed the arm in his twelve-year old hands and ran down the steps setting the object on the table at his familiar seat. Mom was busy bringing hot dishes to the table, assisted by Kristy who was press-ganged into service of filling drinks. Mark sat on his knees on his chair at the table trying to position the fork to fit into the claw.

"Mark, help Kristy bring the drinks to the table please...and get that off the table until dinner's over."

"But I want to show you what I made!" He whined back in protest.

"I would love to see it...after dinner. You know the rules!"

"Yes, Ma'am," Mark set the arm in the corner where it would be safe for the meal and ran into the kitchen narrowly dodging Kristy who was carrying two of the glasses.

They enjoyed a normal family meal with chatter about various things. Mark took the time to explain what his arm was supposed to do, and the family was captive to his enthusiasm showing the required support for the kid in the room.

"Mark! Are you ready?" Eric yelled out into the otherwise empty house.

Mark transported instantly back to reality. He realized how lost he was in the dream, taking a moment to reorient himself.

"Yeah! Be right there!" He yelled back.

He stood up looking once again at the very spot he sat and played so many times, wiped a tear from his eyes, and closed the door behind him.

"Do you have everything?" Eric asked.

"Yes, I have all my chargers and a few more days of clothes over at Debbie's."

ӂ

"Mr. Meyer needs to see you, sir."

"I'll be right up."

Jason set the phone down and grabbed another donut from the box on his desk. Once it was stuffed into his mouth he grabbed his suit coat throwing it over his shoulder and headed out the door to the elevator whistling '*It's a Wonderful Day*'.

The doors opened on Mr. Meyer's floor, and he stepped out, heading to his boss's office. His jacket was now on and the once loose tie was now properly fit. He stopped just outside Mr. Meyer's door to check his mustache for any donut cream remnants before entering.

"Hello, sir," said Jason.

"Come in," Mr. Meyer ordered, "close the door please."

Jason grabbed the chair in the corner dragging it over to be square in front of the large desk. "What's going on?"

"Did you see this?" Mr. Meyer held up a newspaper with images of the crash on the front page.

"I saw it. Another accident. Is it important?" Asked Jason.

"Dr. Jacobs died in the accident."

"Dr. Jacobs?" Jason asked with curiosity as if he was thinking if he knew a Dr. Jacobs, but there was little time to reflect on that question.

"The doctor in charge of the medical team at the hospital?" Mr. Meyer responded with a hint of 'you know that' in his voice.

"Oh, yes," Jason paused looking down, "that's too bad."

"It is. We are sending some money to his wife to help with the arrangements. His contributions to this project were outstanding, and he'll be hard to replace."

"Let's not replace him, sir," Jason stated boldly.

"What do you mean?" Mr. Meyer countered.

"The implant is done. We should be able to handle all the medical things in house at this point."

"Jason, most of the reports need a sign-off from an independent physician. You know that. We'll just interview some people from the team and promote one of them to the lead."

Jason sat back rubbing his mustache. "I have a friend who is a doctor with an independent practice. That makes for a smaller review team, and they are not in a hospital, so there's less chance any reports leaking."

Mr. Meyer leaned back in thought, "Will he need to run his own scans or would he accept ours without question?"

"That's the beauty of it, sir," said Jason, "He does not have a scanner at all; he outsources his scans, but he can use ours scanners for free giving us all the control we need."

"Jason, I am not sure I want to risk changing the teams right now. We are at a critical step in the process and I can't afford to start over."

Jason nodded and leaned back in the chair, "Just think about it, sir."

"I will, but in the meantime, let's hold some interviews from the existing team. I will allow your friend to come into the interview as well. After we do interviews, I'll make my decision. I want to hear from everyone. Until then, your team will need to make sure we have everything up to specifications. Look over all the reports and make sure everything is good to pass along to the next medical team lead."

"I will, sir. We'll go over everything today. Anything else?"

"No. We're done."

Jason stood up, sliding the chair back to the corner where he moved it from. "I'll see you later. Let me know if you need anything else."

Within a few minutes Jason was back at his desk. He picked up his phone and dialed some numbers from memory and spun around in his chair, reaching for another donut.

"Hi Chucky. You got the interview. I'll need to let you know when."

"OK, I know. Yeah."

"Alright. Bye."

29

Eric pulled into Debbie's driveway and stopped the car. The two were mostly silent on the trip from their house, it was a silence that became awkward. Eric let out a tear and a sigh.

"Grab what you need and we will head in."

Mark did not reply. He grabbed the ACAT system, which Eric did not know was in the van.

"Why'd you bring that?"

"I might need it. I'll explain later," said Mark.

"OK," Eric responded with a puzzled expression.

Eric grabbed his bags and the two walked into the front door. Susan was waiting for her husband and gave him an embrace before seeing Mark. She was aghast to see him walking into the house with an exosuit. She looked him up and down in surprise.

"Look at you. You can walk!"

He stood there just holding the old talking machine, but after glancing between everyone in the room, he answered, "It was a difficult project, but we have most of the bugs worked out."

Debbie looked at Mark with a combination of joy and anguish. She was pleased to see joy and movement return to his life, but she believed the cost of that progress was her husband's life. After what seemed too long, she spoke, "Well, let's go look at that letter."

They all followed her into the house and took seats at the large dining room table that usually seated guests at her dinner parties.

"I found this note on John's desk," Debbie said, holding up the envelope displaying words that Eric recognized as coming from his friend's hand. The words were scribbled as though a doctor were filling a prescription:

'If I die...'

"Does this relate to the project?" Mark finally asked quietly.

"We're getting there, Mark," said Eric.

"No, Dad. Is this related to the project!" He was more bold and forceful than usual.

Eric paused for a moment looking at his son, almost as an adult for the first time. "Yes," he finally squeaked, "it is related to the project."

He was expecting his son to protest or get mad, but he never did. "Wait a few minutes before you start," he replied.

Mark stood up from the dinning room chair and slid it to the corner of the room. He retrieved the ACAT computer and rolled the old push wheelchair from the corner of the living room to the table. They all stared at him like he had lost his mind as he sat in the old chair and booted the ACAT. Mark finally pulled the power wire for his suit out of the battery. His arms and legs suddenly went limp, and he sagged in the chair as if his spine just turned to jelly.

"CALL…DAVID." The ACAT finally interjected.

"Mark, it is harder to talk to you like this. Can I get your other speaker from the car?" Asked Susan.

"NO…CALL…DAVID."

"OK, Mark. I'll call. Can we get started first?"

"YES."

Debbie pulled the folded paper out of the envelope. With a deep breath she unfolded the paper and held back some tears. She read the letter slowly to hold back as much emotion as possible.

"If you are reading this letter, it is likely I did not survive. I think someone has been following me for quite some time, and I am sure it is related to the Synaptergy project. The implant cannot be removed and it cannot be turned off. I am one of the few people who knew this. The company has doctored the CT scans to make the reports look more favorable to the public eye. I went along with this so I could stay close to the project to see what was going on. I know there was an anomaly report filed by the robotics team. I am not sure of what all the details are, but I can tell you that Mr. Meyer was just as confused about that report as the rest of us are. This leads me to believe he was not expecting anything of the sort. But someone knows. Someone is able to put thoughts, ideas, choices, into Mark's head, but we do not know who or why. The project is powerful. With it we have seen amazing results, but there is also potential for abuse that could have catastrophic implications. Be careful and figure out this problem. I wish you all my love and luck. John."

They looked around at each other realizing the project went deeper than any of them would have guessed.

"What anomalies?" Susan finally snapped at Mark.

"MUSIC...TASTE," he said.

"I knew about the reports. John and I talked about it, and David sent the details into the company. Mark was following orders and telling me about them."

"CALL...DAVID," Mark finally interjected again, "SHOW...HIM...LETTER."

Eric stood up and walked to the other room. They could only hear half of the conversation but could piece together the rest from the replies. Eric requested David's presence to see the letter himself.

"He will be here in a few minutes," said Eric.

"BATTERY...BELT"

Mark's abbreviated conversation style was familiar to his parents, so they knew he was asking to plug the suit back into the battery pack. Eric was able to slide the adapter back into place and suddenly Mark straightened his posture.

"Why did you turn everything off, Mark?" Susan wanted to know.

"Mom, I'll let David tell you when he gets here," said Mark, "It is too hard to explain on the ACAT and I cannot right now."

Debbie finally stood up and walked over to a wall-mounted television and turned it on. "Let's find something to watch while David is on the way. The conversation's too heavy at the moment."

She flipped the station until she found a sitcom to lighten the mood. They turned their attention to the set where they were absorbed losing all track of time. Suddenly they were jolted from their stupor by the doorbell.

"I'll get it." Mark exclaimed, standing up from his chair.

He opened the front door to find both David and Tyler. They exchanged pleasantries with Mark while walking in.

"Where is everyone?"

"Follow me," Mark said as he led them into the dining area where the television show was still on.

"Hello Eric, Susan." He turned to Debbie, "Hi. I'm David. I am so sorry for your loss."

"Thank you, sir. Please sit down."

"Does everyone know Tyler?" He pointed to his old friend who was also taking a seat.

They greeted him with half-baked unison. He was familiar to Eric and Susan, though Debbie had never met him before.

"I figured I would bring Tyler tonight since he was the one who first noticed some issues with the project. He is the robotics team lead for Synaptergy."

"Thank you, David." He paused, "Sorry we all had to meet like this, and for having to jump right in, but I..." He stopped, patted himself down and grabbed his cell phone from his pocket. "Everyone turn off your phones, and let's set them somewhere else for the time being."

Debbie collected the devices to place them all in another room of the house. Tyler grabbed a small speaker from his pocket and turned it on handing it to Mark. "I know this one is safe, but..." and he shifted his eyes down to the battery pack on his belt. Mark picked up the cue and pulled the battery pack power once again going limp.

"Mark, are you connected?"

"Check," and he heard his voice, "I guess so."

"Great," he paused again, "here's what we know. The implant cannot be removed and cannot be turned off. This information came from John. We also know that the scans in the reports are doctored, but we don't know how. The device is capable of receiving signals in addition to sending them, but we don't have any information about what the implant does when it receives the data. The hardware suggests close range connections or wireless connections could both send data to the implant through certain hardware. We only have three hardware devices that only receive data, all the other ones send data to the implant. Putting all this together, I know someone can send signals into Mark's mind which causes these changes in his personality, preferences, and possibly other factors we have not yet considered."

"Today we installed some logging software to track things coming and going from the speaker." David chimed in, "I had a chance to look over the logs briefly. Not sure if you have yet, Mark."

"No, I did not have a chance. What did you find?"

"There are a few words there you might be familiar with: *Florida Georgia Line, Late Nate News,* and *Strawberry.*"

"Strawberry?" Susan asked.

"The nasty flavor of today?" Mark causally answered, "Tyler, why would someone want to manipulate my desires?"

"I know why," Debbie finally offered, "I have spent a long time in marketing. We are always trying to find new ways to convince people to buy products. This could be a way to increase marketing effectiveness."

"Maybe," Eric added, "But what if it's more than that? Sure, a new product line or brand could pop up and make someone millions overnight, and that would be a good plan to become wealthy, but what about power?"

"Power, Dad?"

"Yes," He stopped to breathe and think about the things he was saying, "What if people could be influenced to change their votes? If enough people have this implant, the fabric of society could be shifted to the whims of its controller! Laws could change–entire ideas. What would that do to our world?"

Eric paused, thinking to himself about what he was saying. In the natural conversational lull, Mark casually glanced to the television screen, "Turn up the volume!" He shouted through the speaker.

Everyone's head darted in the direction of the television screen to see the Synaptergy logo just fading away to a man sitting at a computer. Debbie quickly turned up the television volume and they all watched,

"Imagine if you could increase your productivity ten-fold! Our new device, safely implanted so you never lose it, can increase the speed you use your computer, open up your doors, even start your car! No more keys, or typing, or mouse clicks. If you can think it, you can control it! Contact us at Synaptergy for more details about how you can make your life more productive."

The commercial ended and they looked around the room. Mark looked down at his wrecked body, unable to control himself without this implant, the same implant that could allow persons unknown to control his thoughts.

"Is it worth it?"

"What, Mark?"

"Is it worth using this technology to walk, if I am walking into a world I cannot control? If this is sold around the world, it could change everything! Is it worth changing the whole world so a few of us can walk again?"

"Mark, these are hard questions. And we will answer them by walking together." David put his hand on Mark's limp shoulder and the boy mustered a hard-won smile.

ACKNOWLEDGEMENTS

Thanks to the many people who have helped to bring this project to fruition. To Tyler, for cover photography and early comments and direction on the story and manuscript. Also, to Dale and Sammy for making additional early comments on the draft.

The beta reader team also provided numerous alterations and suggestions during the early editing phases, and thanks to Kate for editorial comments and suggestions on clarity surrounding some of the industries we talked about in this book.

Thanks for Vince for taking some of the audio production load to finalize the audiobook edition to help us reach out deadline.

ABOUT THE AUTHOR

Thomas Murosky has worked as a freelance technology consultant focusing on Internet privacy, FOSS software, and web design since 2010 after leaving academia. Since that time, he has founded a small Indie press where he publishes Christian, self-help, and Christian titles. Tom is also the author behind the SwitchedToLinux brand which has helped several people understand the power of free and open source software in regular work routines.

Thomas Murosky has also written the following:

Science Fiction -
    Lockdown

Christian -
    Testing and Temptations
    The Art of Shallow Neighboring
    I AM not amused
    Josiah's Sanctification
    Happy Hellidays
    Hezekiah's Prayer